AUGUSTOWN

Kei Miller was born in Jamaica in 1978. He is the author of two novels, *The Same Earth* and *The Last Warner Woman*, several collections of poetry and a book of short stories, *Fear of Stones*, which was shortlisted for the Commonwealth Writers' Prize for Best First Book. In 2014, he won the prestigious Forward Prize for Poetry for his collection, *The Cartographer Tries to Map a Way to Zion*. He teaches creative writing at Royal Holloway, University of London.

Follow Kei @keimiller or visit his website:
www.underthesaltireflag.com

AUGUSTOWN

Kei Miller

WEIDENFELD & NICOLSON

First published in Great Britain in 2016
by Weidenfeld & Nicolson,
an imprint of the Orion Publishing Group Ltd
Carmelite House, 50 Victoria Embankment
London EC4Y 0DZ

An Hachette UK Company

1 3 5 7 9 10 8 6 4 2

Acknowledgement is made for permission to reprint an excerpt from
The Dictionary of Place-Names in Jamaica by Inez Knibb Sibley.
Used herewith by permission of the Institute of Jamaica.

A CIP catalogue record for this book is
available from the British Library.

978 1 474 60359 1 (cased)
978 1 474 60360 7 (export trade paperback)

Typeset by Input Data Services Ltd, Bridgwater, Somerset

Printed in Great Britain by Clays Ltd, St Ives plc

Note:

The events of this novel take place in the fictional valley of Augustown — a community that bears an uncanny resemblance to and shares a parallel history with a very real place: August Town, Jamaica.

August Town, in the hills of St. Andrew, Jamaica is thought to have been named from the fact that freedom came to the enslaved people of this country on 'Augus Mawnin' — the 1st August, 1838. August Town later became notable because at this place a prophet, whose name was Bedward, arose. He had thousands of followers, but outdid himself when he proclaimed that he was God and could fly.

from The Dictionary of Place-Names in Jamaica

Contents

The Flying Preacherman

♦

First you must imagine the sky, blue and cloudless if that helps, or else the luminously black spread of night. Next – and this is the important bit – you must imagine yourself inside it. Inside the sky, floating beside me. Below us, the green and blue disc of the earth.

Now focus. 17° 59' 0" North, 76° 44' 0" West. Down there is the Caribbean, though not the bits you might have seen in a pretty little brochure. We are beyond the aquamarine waters, with their slow manatees and graceful sea turtles, and beyond the beaches littered with sweet almonds. We have gone inland. Down there is a dismal little valley on a dismal little island. Notice the hills, how one of them carries on its face a scar – a section where bulldozers and tractors have sunk their rusty talons into its cheeks, scraped away the brush and the trees and left behind a white crater of marl. The eyesore can be seen from ten or more miles away. To the people who live in this valley, it feels as if they wear the scar on their own skin – as if a kind of ruin has befallen them.

Seen from up here, the ramshackle valley looks like a pot of cornmeal porridge, rusting tin roofs stirred into its hot, bubbling vortex. Perhaps it is the dust bowls, the tracts of sand and the dry riverbed that give the place this cornmeally look. The streets run in unplanned and sometimes maze-like directions; paved roads often thin into dirt paths; wide streets narrow into alleys lined with zinc or scrap-board fences. If solid concrete houses rise like sentinels at the beginning of a road, the architecture will devolve into clumsy board shacks by the time you get to the cul-de-sac. If on one road the houses are separated into tidy lots, on the road just over they are crowded together and lean into each other as if for comfort. This is a community that does not quite come together.

We must imagine there was a time when all of this was beautiful and unscarred; a time when the hills were whole and green – verdant humps rolling up towards the Blue Mountain range above; a time when the valley was thick with guava trees, when wild parakeets flew above the forest and fat iguanas sunbathed on river-smoothed rocks. But that is all we can do. Imagine. There is no forest any more, and no more iguanas, and the mineral river that once flowed swiftly through the valley is now dammed up, its waters diverted to the city's reservoir. Where there was once a perfect green hill, there is now a scar, and where there was once a river, there is now just a dry riverbed, little boys playing football among its vast sands. Where there once was beauty, now there is just 'Augustown', or sometimes 'Greater Augustown' if you listen to the island's city officials, who have

4

seen fit to attach to it, like addendums, the nearby districts of Kintyre, Rockers, Bryce Hill, Dread Heights and 'Gola.

Down there it is 11 April 1982, a day I have watched over and over again, as if from up here I could change things; could slip inside its hours and change the outcome. But I can only watch.

For here is the truth: each day contains much more than its own hours, or minutes, or seconds. In fact, it would be no exaggeration to say that every day contains all of history.

◆

1

Blind people hear and taste and smell what other people cannot, and what Ma Taffy smells on this early afternoon makes her sit up straight. She smells it high and ripe and stink on the air, like a bright green jackfruit in season being pulled to the rocky ground below. The smell is coming down John Golding Road right alongside the boy-child, something attached to him, like a spirit but not quite.

She has been hearing him for a while now – all the sniffling, hiccuping, short-of-breath sounds. But it is not the crying that makes Ma Taffy alert. There is nothing special in this. The old woman is used to the little boy coming from school wet-eyed and vexed with the world for whatever injustice he feels has befallen him this time. 'A backbone,' she often thinks to herself. 'That little boy is in need of a backbone.' He has stopped crying now, yet something is still coming to the house with him. Something with a smell, so Ma Taffy is paying careful attention.

A spliff glows idly between her fingers. She has abandoned it for the moment. She continues, however, to draw in breath after breath with the same slow deliberateness, holding onto it, trying to separate the things she knows from the things she does not know. She knows, for instance, the various smells of herself: the dull flavour of ganja fresh on her breath, the carbolic soap she washed with earlier and, underneath that, her own old woman smells. She knows the smell of the wooden house behind her, of the zinc fence rusting slowly, of the chicken coop round back and even the smell of each of the five hens separate from the rank smell of the rooster; she can smell the mangoes and the cherries and the otaheite apples ripening together, and then all the vague but distinct everyday smells of Augustown: coal fires burning, turn cornmeal turning, crack rice boiling, the sweat of blackwomen standing over pots, the sweat of blackmen standing in the streets. And then there it is, behind all of it, something else. A smell slightly sour, but tight and choking like – like rats!

Irie Tafari, otherwise known as Ma Taffy, is almost always calmly disposed, but the thought of rats makes her twitch. It was over ten years ago; they had been breeding in the roof – a whole colony, rat mama and rat papa having plenty rat pickney and those plenty rat pickney having even more rat pickney – and it had created that smell, thin and sour and choking. There were the nightly scuttling sounds and, before long, rat shit started to drizzle around the house like a small, intermittent rain.

Ma Taffy should have known long before the terrible thing happened that it was going to happen. On that night she had been dreaming of a whistling sound. It was all around her. The whistling grew into a moaning. She opened her eyes but it was so dark that she couldn't see the ever-expanding belly of the ceiling, how it was creakily reaching towards her. But she heard, above the moaning, the frantic rats shrieking, hissing, swearing, chattering. The roof gave out with a pop and she finally saw them – hundreds of the snake-tailed rodents falling towards her, scrabbling the air, their beady eyes shining red in the dark. Strange, Ma Taffy sometimes thinks, how a coming autoclaps had made her open her eyes wide in anticipation instead of closing them for protection.

The rats gouged out one eye completely and badly damaged the other. If she tips her head to a certain angle, and looks out of the lower portion, she can manage to see a shadowy grey world. But this takes so much effort and reveals so little that Ma Taffy hardly does so. Instead she has grown used to the darkness.

Ma Taffy lifts the spliff back to her mouth. She is growing nervous. Another coming autoclaps. 'Steady your heart, Taffy,' she whispers to herself. 'Steady.'

Ma Taffy is already the great expert of steadiness. This is the woman who sits in the selfsame spot where she is sitting now, no matter how the world tilts around her. She once sat there during a whole hurricane. And even worse, whenever the badmen and rudeboys of Augustown are trading bullets with Babylon or with themselves, while almost everyone else in Augustown is locked tight inside their houses, Ma Taffy just sits out there, steady, steady, blinking her useless eyes.

Two years earlier, when the newly formed Angola Gang found themselves under siege by the police, Ma Taffy did even more than just stay outside. She stood up, reached for her cane and walked down the stairs of her verandah. She walked straight into the middle of the road and into the line of fire. At once, the bullets stopped.

Ma Taffy stood regal in the road. Her dreadlocks were piled on top of her head, a green and yellow turban wrapped around them. She knew that from their hiding place the Angola Boys were watching her, confused, and that from another hiding place the police were also watching, probably making desperate hand gestures.

Ma Taffy alone was steady and sure. She walked just a few hundred yards over to the half-built house that had been abandoned years ago, it probably having occurred to the owners that if one had enough money to build a house, then one had enough money to leave Augustown. Thick cerasee vines now grew through the concrete, drawing the structure back into the vegetation. Ma Taffy stepped through the open doorway and five rudeboys looked up, their faces suddenly softened by a kind of innocence. They were just boys, after all, though they tried not to let this show. One of them, no more than seventeen, shook himself out of his embarrassment and addressed Ma Taffy. 'Old woman, what you come here for? Go back to yu house.'

Ma Taffy turned her face towards the voice. Her yellowed eye found the face it wanted and seemed to scrutinise it.

After a moment the man-boy added, more respectfully, 'Please, Ma Taffy. It not safe out here.'

The old woman remained silent. There were many things she was being careful not to say and yet, in the quiet of the moment, the shadow of these things passed clearly between herself and the man-boy.

'Listen bwoy, who not too long ago was still sucking milk from him momma titty – don't pass your place with me.' Ma Taffy's lips weren't moving, and yet the man-boy was hearing the old woman's voice in his head. Her voice continued: 'I understand them calling you Soft-Paw now – and maybe, maybe that is right. Maybe every boy-pickney when him get

10

to a certain age should have a say in him own name, cause he don't get to choose much else in this life. But Marlon is the name me know you as since you was just a lickle-bitty boy running up to my verandah, hiding behind mi skirt from your momma long belt.'

Ma Taffy paused and swallowed, and then the shadow of the unsaid things grew thicker and darker. 'Listen. Mi know what them did do to Petey. Mi know how for the past two months him was doing yard work for a woman who live up in Hope Pastures. Mi know how this woman must did get it into her head that him tief money from off her table and that she call Babylon to report him. From that same verandah over there I sit and hear everything – I hear when Babylon come into Augustown the night, the sound of them jeeps like they was crushing more than just the stones on the road. They stop in front of the rum-bar, go inside and drag Petey out – Petey who was already so deep under him whites that he never understand what was going on. And I hear how them address him, *Dutty yard bwoy! What you do with the woman money?* This was the new corporal boy, a tall mawga fellow who so mawga that if he turn sideways you almost don't see him at all. Is him who take out the rifle and use the butt and koof Petey hard on him head, so hard that Petey fall to the ground and blood start run down him face and same time he get sober. This tall, mawga corporal, like maybe he trying to prove just how big and bad him is, getting more irate for no reason at all. He start to shout at Petey, *Tell me right now what you do wid de woman raasclawt money!* And Petey now just shaking him head, the blood dripping from him forehead into him eye, and him just saying the same thing over and over, calm-like, trying not to cause no trouble, *Mi nuh know nothing* bout money, officer. Mi nuh take nobody money. This corporal bwoy then spit on the ground and him lean over and push him face right up to Petey. You is a fucking tief! he whisper. Petey say again, with a little more strength this time, Mi a nuh tief! and he begin to reach into him pocket. It happen so quick, the corporal bwoy raise him rifle, turn it round, and . . . and Petey's head explode like a bright green jackfruit that fall and buss on the ground below. They strap Petey's body to the front of the jeep as if him was nothing but a wild hog they catch up in Blue Mountain, and they drive round Augustown. And you might remember, Soft-Paw, how we was all so quiet then, but Babylon never understand that ours was the quiet of old and hungry tigers who wondering if they maybe have the strength to pounce. Cause if Babylon did understand that, then them woulda know to look a little bit scared as well, and them woulda wonder, maybe, if them did really have the muscle to fight we off if we did pounce. They drive out at last, and take Petey with them.

'Soft-Paw, mi know is you did go out into the road later that night and find the wallet that Petey was reaching into him pocket for, and when you open it there was nothing more than the five dollars the woman from Hope Pastures did pay him for the work him did do. Not a thing more. But we hear it on radio, the selfsame story that Babylon always decide fi tell – how them come into Augustown to look for a known criminal, how the criminal open fire pon them, and how them did return fire and kill him. You say that this thing don't concern old people like me, but that is only cause you still talking with titty milk in yu mouth, excuse mi language. Lickle bwoy, you too young. You don't know fully the fight you involved in and how long it been going on for. What you fighting is Babylon system, all them things in this life that put a heavy stone on the heads of people like you and me – all them things that cause we not to rise. Chu, some of we been fighting that fight a long, long time now.'

When the shadow of these things had finished passing between the two, the man-boy trembled a little. Ma Taffy turned her yellow eye away and said aloud for the first time a simple instruction: 'Follow me.'

'Listen, old woman . . .' Soft-Paw began to protest, but Ma Taffy was already walking towards the back of the house, stepping through another open doorway, this one leading towards the river. Soft-Paw shook his head but followed. 'I soon come back,' he whispered to the others.

Soft-Paw had earned his name because of how lightly he was able to step. Soft like a cat, materialising in front of people like a ghost. And yet, soft and soundless as he was able to move, the blind woman moved even softer. As they went around the circumference of Augustown, Soft-Paw fought to keep up. They had walked almost a mile before the old woman stopped. 'You know where you deh?'

'Yes, Ma Taffy.'

'Willy's corner shop perch just up there above us. Inside you will find the tall, mawga corporal.' She lowered her face and spat. 'Raasclawt coward not even have the courage fi be where the other Babylon boys is fighting the fight weh him start.'

The old woman was quiet for a moment and then said, 'Go and do what you done decide you have to do.'

Soft-Paw pulled the gun from where he had stuffed it into the back of his pants. His waistband slapped against his taut and muscular back. He seemed to weigh the gun between his hands, and for the second time that day he was a child again, the weight of his decision pressing down on him. Ma Taffy started to say something but stopped. She knew she had to allow him to be a man and a warrior in his own way. She turned and walked back the same way she had come from. Soft-Paw slunk up to the corner shop.

Ma Taffy hadn't walked for a minute before the retort of the Glock seemed to suck all the silence out of the world. She felt the sound in every wrinkle of her face, and then she felt it in her chest. She stopped where she was. In a moment the grass behind her was being trampled. Soft-Paw was no longer taking soft steps. He was running. She heard his ragged breaths and felt the wind as he ran past.

It was a hot day. Even without being able to see, Ma Taffy knew that the Mona River was so low it was not flowing. It was, instead, a series of stagnant ponds from which mosquitoes were hatching every second. She felt the insects around her face and her arms. She heard them in her ears. She took a breath and continued, steady, steady back to her house.

This is the Ma Taffy I have always known. Nothing ever rattles her. So it is strange that on this afternoon, lifting her head to the wind, she is instructing herself to stay calm.

The smell is thick now. She knows the little boy is turning into the yard, climbing the steps onto the verandah towards her.

'Where Mommy deh?' he asks.

It is a useless question. The boy already knows that his mother, Gina, is at work. This is not the point of his question, and Ma Taffy understands that. He wants his mother,

14

who will stand up for him, who will protect and avenge him, not Ma Taffy who will tell him no nonsense about backbone and how important it is to stand up on his own.

Gina has inherited Ma Taffy's backbone and knows how to stand up to her, and anybody who knows how to stand up to Ma Taffy can stand up to anyone. This is what Kaia has reasoned in his own mind. This is why he wants his mother right now. When the gunfights break out in Augustown, Gina is not pleased. While Ma Taffy will sit quietly on the verandah, Gina will walk up and down in a great agitation. The guns in the distance will pop – bap-bap-bap – while her rubber sandals go clip-clop, clip-clop. The clip-clops pause, then build again, pause, then build again – their cadences finally reaching a full explosion. 'What gunfighting ever do to solve anything? Tell me that, Auntie! What they really think all of this going to do? Them so fucking short-sighted – the whole lot of them. Not one ounce of good any of this warring go-ing to do except kill we off.'

Ma Taffy would have been waiting for this, and would now turn her head towards Gina. 'They doing what they feel them haffi do, child. Defending us. You could have lickle . . . eem . . .'

'Sympathy?' Gina would offer, because even though in these discussions they were adversaries, it remained her duty to supply the old woman with words whenever she couldn't find them.

'Yes. Thank you,' Ma Taffy would say. 'That is the word I looking for. You could have lickle sympathy for what them doing out there.'

'Nobody ever come and ask me if I need defending. I don't need protection from no gunman.'

'Not everybody can be like you, Gina.'

She is a force of nature, this Gina, smart and headstrong, and so Ma Taffy understands why the boy wants to see her now. But the boy's mother will not be back for another hour or two, so Ma Taffy pats the spot on the bench right beside her. 'Come, lickle boy,' she says, 'Come siddung beside your Grandma.'

In fact, she is the boy's great-aunt, but in this household and to everyone in Augustown, it seems an unnecessary distinction to make.

The boy sits. The old woman sniffs the air again and almost gags. She puts a hand on the boy's knee. Kaia makes a whimpering sound and draws very close to her, his head now resting on the old woman's shoulder. Ma Taffy decides it is not yet time to ask, *What is the matter? Who trouble you?* She knows that whatever is going to happen, whatever is going to pour out into the world, it will pour out soon enough. It will happen, as certain as the midnight rain of rats. And if she can hold it off for just a little longer, she will. So instead she asks a question that surprises even herself as she asks it.

'Kaia, I ever tell you bout the flying preacherman?'

Kaia looks up. For a small moment he forgets about the day. For just a small moment, his newly dulled eyes shimmer again. He shakes his head. He feels the afternoon breeze soft and light on his scalp.

'No.' He pouts the word over a thumb he has been sucking. 'You never tell me no story like that before.'

'Well, well, well,' Ma Taffy says, sitting back and returning the spliff to her mouth. She exhales a cloud of ganja that envelops herself and the boy. She turns her face towards the scarred hillside as if the story she is about to tell exists there. 'Shame on me. Every lickle yute from Augustown ought to know the story of the flying preacherman.'

2

The distant past comes back to us, usually, as a shock – an echo that has escaped its own fleetingness – that has widened so wide and so quickly, we have slipped inside it without being ready. It comes, then, as a panic in the heart, a widening of the eyes, an 'O' of the mouth. In the days of the flying preacherman, Ma Taffy was the same age that Kaia is now. It does not surprise her that she was once a little girl; it surprises her only that she is now so many years away from that time.

'In them there long-ago days, there was a church here in Augustown,' Ma Taffy says, as if from far away. 'They called it Union Camp. It was a church for poor people, but they build the chapel bigger than hospital, and with walls that was clean as Dettol. So you can imagine that Babylon was fraid of this church. Them did fraid of it like puss. Poor people build the church right down here in the valley, but to Babylon's eyes it was like the church was already on top of Mount Zion. The stones they use to build the church was big and white and in the shape of diamonds. It was over three hundred strapping men who form a line from the river all the way to the church building site, and they pass the stones from hand to hand. That's how we did work in

18

them long-ago days. But yes, is the preacherman I want to tell you bout, the preacherman who did in charge of that very church. Him was a very special man. Yes. Very special.'

Ma Taffy sighs. 'Is plenty years now that him dead. They bury him in the graveyard close by the church – the place I hear people call *Duppy Lane* these days.'

Kaia shivers a little and pulls himself closer to this woman he thinks of as his grandmother. Like everyone in Augustown, he knows the Bedward Graveyard, and like everyone under the age of ten, he is afraid of that place. He wonders if it is a duppy story his grandma is about to tell him. After all, men can't fly, but duppies definitely can.

'The preacherman's name was Alexander Bedward, and is him who did tell we one day that him was going to fly.'

Kaia's eyes flicker over a memory but then they fall flat. He pouts his disappointment. 'I know this story already.' He takes his thumb from his mouth and begins to sing a song he has learnt at school. '*Guess what? Bedward jump, and Bedward bruck him neck! Bedward jump, and Bedward bruck him neck!*'

Ma Taffy grips her cane and brings it down hard on the wooden deck of the verandah. 'You was there?!' she asks through gritted teeth.

Kaia stops and resumes his sulking. He is not used to this kind of tone from his grandma.

'Mi ask if you was there,' Ma Taffy insists.

'No,' Kaia whispers, 'I never did dere.'

'Well then, hush up you blasted mout and don't try fi tell me things that you don't even know, or things that Babylon decide fi tell you.'

The old woman swallows. She wonders why this little song has made her so upset this afternoon, and why she should take it out on Kaia. He is just being his usual little-boyish self. She counsels herself with even more firmness, 'Steady, old woman! What wrong with you today?'

It is a quiet afternoon, but the kind of quiet that is full of everyday sounds. There is wind in the tall breadfruit trees and in the shorter croton plants; the mongrel dogs of Augustown are calling to and answering each other; radios are on in every house and so the cantankerous talk show host, Mutty Perkins, is in a kind of chorus with himself; and in another lane not far away, it sounds as if Mr Desmond is once again having brutal sex with his common-law wife, Monica, for there is the distinct sound of the banging zinc, and behind it, Monica shouting every conceivable profanity; so much so that Augustown is growing humid with her curse words. Sometimes Mr Desmond and Monica's carrying-ons really do grow frighteningly loud, Monica screaming out 'Murder!' or 'Him a guh kill mi!', but even on such occasions no one dares intervene because past experience has taught them that Monica herself will march out, completely naked, her eyes swollen, and yet still she will hurl stones at whoever has interrupted her and her man, telling them point blank, 'Cockroack nuh business inna fowl fight!'

Suddenly, another woman shouts from a house in the same lane, 'Come nuh, man! Come nuh! I waiting on you!'

Ma Taffy frowns. This is Sister Gilzene, of course, one of the oldest living persons in Augustown, a childless spinster who for months now has been losing her mind, waiting on death and calling it upon herself. Every day she can be heard half praying and half cursing on the mattress from which she can no longer rise. 'Stupid old woman,' Ma Taffy says, though there is a sympathy in her voice that does not quite match the harshness of her words. She was there as well, Ma Taffy now remembers. All of sixty-two years ago Sister Gilzene was there.

'Grandma. Tell me the story,' Kaia says.

Ma Taffy stands up as if to be by herself. 'Bedward did fly,' she whispers at last. 'He did really fly.'

And then she gasps. For here it is, the small panic of the heart, the widening of the eyes, the 'O' of the mouth. O! O! O! The past!

Before she changed her name by deed poll to Irie Tafari, which in due course was shortened to Miss Taffy, which in due course (with the onset of silver hair, wrinkles and the three nieces she looked after, becoming their virtual mother), was further shortened to Ma Taffy, she had had another name: Irene McKenzie. She had lived with her mother and a man who, it had been explained to her, was not quite her father, but rather the gentleman with whom her mother, Norah, was 'in conversation'. That is how such things were said in those days. The ongoing 'conversation' between Miss Norah and her gentleman, Maas Bilby, eventually produced three daughters, Irene's younger sisters, who would all move away from Augustown when they were older, but who would each, after they felt they had already produced their allotted portion of children, send the last surprise fruits of their womb off to Augustown to grow up with their ageing aunt. And so this is how, without ever having given birth herself, Ma Taffy ended up mothering Tisha and Beverley and Gina. Indeed, Ma Taffy imagines the three girls as her own daughters, and the three girls, though they are technically cousins, imagine each other as sisters.

21

Ma Taffy remembers her mother's gentleman, Maas Bilby, as a man with a broad face and an even broader smile. He had worked variously as a cowherder on the Papine Estate, as a field man, as a saddler and as a mason, but his most consistent work was as a petty thief, which is why he was never able to keep the other jobs, which, in any case, did not pay him as much as his occasional larceny. His long bouts of unemployment led to intense bickering in the house – heated conversations between himself and Norah. And yet, Maas Bilby was a man of certain principles. He made it a point to go out every morning – whatever the nature of the work, legal or illegal – and to come home each evening before it was fully dark. And although he stole, Maas Bilby tithed a portion of all his earnings to the church. By rights, he should never have been called 'Maas Bilby', but simply 'Bilby'. The respectable title was not usually assigned to those who persisted in such disrespectable careers as his. And yet, through his own will and his own vision of himself, which were strong enough to bend people to his way of seeing, and also through the sheer breadth of his chest, which sometimes seemed to take up the whole road when he was out walking, it seemed impossible to call him simply 'Bilby'. So he was 'Maas', and everyone accepted him as the most respectable thief in Augustown.

Maas Bilby used to play a game when he got home in the evenings. He would take a deep breath, close his eyes tight and then try to identify what had been cooked for dinner. Opening his eyes at last, and smiling his broad smile, he would sit down at the table and say, 'I wonder what it is my good, good woman has cooked today. I hope it is . . .' and here he would identify the dish which Norah had indeed cooked.

Norah played along, and often tried to make it difficult. She put things into the pot that were not supposed to go together. In this way, she had stumbled upon creative cooking, and frequently dished out a kind of gourmet fare. Norah it was who made curried oranges and beef; who invented sardine rundown; and who made up what would eventually become her most famous soup: fish and ackee in a coconut broth. But for such a big man, Maas Bilby's nose was delicate and discerning. He could detect things hidden under things, and so he almost always guessed right. When he did, he would lift his head to the sky and roar good-naturedly, 'Laawwd, what a blessing of a woman is this, fi know exactly what my mind did give me to eat today!'

On the day that Bedward began to rise, Ma Taffy would always remember, Maas Bilby had said his mind had given him to eat stew peas.

'I wonder what my good, good woman has cooked for me today,' he had said, sitting down and sniffing the air. The smell of stew peas was so obvious that he sniffed the air again, wondering if he had missed something. No. It really was only stew peas. One of his favourite dishes. He smiled. 'I really hope it is stew peas! Stew peas with a piece of pig's tail in it. Yes. That is exactly what my mind give me to eat today.'

Norah walked to the table with a mound of steaming white rice. On top of it was the purple spread of stew peas. From the corner where she was sitting quietly, Irene saw that her mother had dished the meal out on one of her 'good plates' – a broad blue and white dish with the king's insignia in the middle. Norah then poured Maas Bilby a generous portion of coconut water – not in his usual black-rimmed enamel cup, but in the special glass she liked to call her 'good crystal'.

Maas Bilby was quiet and eyed Norah through the slant of his eyes as he shovelled three tablespoons of the food immediately into his mouth. Norah shifted her weight from foot to foot. She wrung her hands.

'Anything else you want?' she stuttered.

Maas Bilby nodded, but it took him a while to swallow the hot food. Rolling his neck like a snake, the food finally went down into his gullet and he spoke. 'I want one more thing. I want you fi tell me whatever it is you have on your mind fi tell me. Norah, if you ever see yourself, is like you almost ready to burs'.'

'Chu man!' Nora said dismissively, as if to be coy, but then she shook herself and pulled up a chair beside Maas Bilby. Maas Bilby was surprised at the quickness of this, and indeed it was in this way that Little Irene understood that the thing her mother was about to say was important. Irene waited then for the inevitable – for her mother or for Maas Bilby to look over to the corner where she was sitting and instruct her to leave the room. She was used to being dismissed whenever adults were speaking. 'We is having a big people's conversation!' they would tell her. 'Go and find something else to do. Your ears too small for this.' But Irene was not dismissed, and she wondered for a short while if it meant that she was officially a big person. She decided, however, just to be safe, that she would remain very, very quiet with her ears wide, wide open.

'Something strange been happening to Master Bedward,' Norah began. 'Is Sister Liz who come here earlier today and tell me herself, and you know she is not the kind to gossip. Especial not bout her own husband.'

24

It was an understatement. Sister Liz was the kind of woman who seemed to make it a point not to say anything at all. She usually spoke only with her eyes, which were aloof and judgemental. That she had come to the house to confide in Norah must have meant this was serious business indeed.

'So, what kind of strange we talking?' Bilby asked.

'The strangest of strange. I will tell you how Sister Liz tell me. She say that she wake up at an unknown hour yessiday night because a cool breeze from the river did come into the bedroom. She say it was a sharp, sharp breeze like it did want to freeze off her two legs. She never even think to open her eyes and look. She just reach over for the piece of sheet that she usual share with Bedward. But no matter how she was patting down the bed, her hands couldn't find no sheet. She reach over little further to touch her husband, but she couldn't find him neither. It was then that she open her eyes and try to see in the dark. She say she was getting real confused, for though she could hear him snoring close by, like him was still beside her, she didn't see him none at all. She even start to wonder if at his big horse-steering age him manage to roll off the bed like some little pickney. Well, she look over the left side and then she look over the right side, but him wasn't there. At last she look up to the ceiling, and that's where him was.'

'In the ceiling?!'

'Yes. Up in the ceiling.'

'Then is climb him climb up there?'

'No. That is the strange thing. Him was just floating. Anancy cobwebs did wrap up all bout his face, and the bed sheets did still wrap round his body.'

'That gone beyond strange,' Maas Bilby muttered, the stew peas now all but forgotten.

'Sister Liz tell me that she had was to creep out of the bedroom. She was trying not to wake him up. She get her two grown boys to come and help her. The three of them had to pull him down real gentle, cause maybe if he wake up too sudden he just fall and bruck his neck.'

'That is what happen when people float in the air?'

'Who to tell? You can't take no risk with these things. You have to be careful.'

'So he stay on the bed for the rest of the night?'

'More or less, it seem. Liz say she still see that he was floating a little, but him never go all the way up to the ceiling again. And in any case, she make sure to keep her hands round him for the rest of the night. Come morning now, and Bedward begin to notice it himself. He complain that he was feeling real light – a feeling like he didn't have any weight on him at all. Sister Liz had to tell him with the straightest face – *my dear husband, is because you have begun to float*.'

'Jesus, Father!' Maas Bilby whispered. 'What all this could mean, though?'

Norah was silent for a moment. 'I don't know, Bilby. I been thinking bout it all day and I don't know . . .'

'Floating! *Sons of war arise, sons of war arise*,' he hummed the chorus a little. 'Don't that was the song we was singing in church yesterday?'

Norah smiled at him.

'What a thing, though, eeh? To float like feather. Or like Ezekiel lifted up into the chariot. It must mean something good!' Maas Bilby enthused, but his face immediately became less sure. 'Don't you think so, Norah?' He asked this with a great earnestness, and, for all his bulk, he seemed almost boyish at this moment. 'Don't it must mean something good?'

Norah bit her lip and observed the man who, despite her best efforts, she continued to love. She knew the kind of redemption he was looking for. He was a man who had made mistakes and was forever looking for a fresh start. She held his hand and spoke the words as if her speaking would make them so. 'I think so, Bilby. All day I been trying not to think so, but in my heart of hearts that is what I think. It must mean something good.'

'Like maybe,' Maas Bilby said, his own heart swelling once again, 'it mean the stone finally going to roll off of our heads.'

Stone?!

Irene didn't realise she had said the word out loud. She was surprised at the sound of her own small voice. Norah and Maas Bilby were now looking at her. She wanted to take it back immediately, but her mother simply nodded. 'The stone that poor people like us born with, Irene. Is a stone that sit right on top of our heads. The one that always stop we from rising.'

Irene nodded her own head, pretending to understand.

'So what Master Bedward going to do now?' Maas Bilby asked.

Norah turned back to the gentleman she was in conversation with. 'Sister Liz say that he giving himself over to prayer and fasting. She leave him there in the room in deep concentration, reading his Bible. Him was already halfway to the ceiling and like him don't even notice. He tell her before she leave that he going to stay in that room praying

27

and only drinking water, until he understand exactly what is happening to him. That's why she was stopping by every house. She asking us to pray for him in such a time as this.'

Maas Bilby stood up then, suddenly and a little awkward-ly, rolling his shoulders like a man preparing for a fight. 'Well, maybe we should do that right now. We should pray for him.' Maas Bilby looked over to the corner where Irene was still staring. 'You come over here too and take our hands. You is part of this.'

Irene walked over and joined the circle of prayer, and in-deed it is true what they would say, years later, that all over Augustown even thieves were praying for Bedward. Now, sixty years later, Ma Taffy can still feel those hands, and how it had seemed to her that their texture was also the texture of prayer – coarse and trembling, warm and sure.

'You see, Kaia,' Ma Taffy says, 'when Bedward tell us that him going to fly, it wasn't because his head did suddenly take him. It wasn't because he did start to believe no non-sense that he was God. It was because he really did begin to fly. I telling you this because I did see it for myself. With my own two eyes I did see it.'

When the past takes hold of us, it does not let go easily. We find ourselves, miraculously, in two places at once. And be-cause Ma Taffy is blind, it is easier for her to shut out much of the world around her. The sun is still shining down on Augustown; the dogs are still barking; and the radios are still loud with the voice of Mutty Perkins. But Ma Taffy remains in the past.

She takes the weight off of her walking stick and eases her body back down to the seat behind her. Almost absent-mindedly she reaches a hand out to rub Kaia's head. Upon touching it, her hand grows cold and begins to tremble. She withdraws it. It is in this way – the touching of Kaia's head – that Ma Taffy is ushered fully and violently back into the present. Yet because she now knows something of the shape of the approaching storm, the nature of the autoclaps, she is able to find within herself a place of calm. She asks her grandson in a careful and measured way, 'Who has done this to you, boy? Tell me now.'

She asks it so calmly that Kaia forgets to cry or blubber as he had been doing earlier. He reports the simple, dry-eyed truth. 'Is the teacher, Grandma. Is Mr Saint-Josephs who cut off my dreadlocks.'

3

Little as they're told, there are stories of men, and sometimes women, who have started from the ground of Augustown and who have risen up, up into the air as if they were floating. Some of these are wonderful, others are tragic, but mostly they are a little bit of both. And usually, these are not what you would call 'history'. No. These are just old-time stories – things that have never been written down and that live only in the recesses of people's minds, people who barely want to remember them, let alone speak them. Still, the stories bounce against each other like echoes.

Take, for instance, this old-time story:

There was once a gentleman who walked through Augustown on an afternoon that was not particular in any way other than the way in which he would make it particular.

That day the sun squatted itself in the middle of a white cloud so that it seemed as though a poached egg were floating in the sky. The gentleman took slow and measured steps. His hands were thrust deep into the pockets of his well-worn khaki trousers. His hands were thrust deep into his pockets, because overnight those hands had developed a tremble and it was spreading to his entire body, so by keeping his hands in his pockets, the man was trying to hide the fact of this.

On this day that was not yet particular but soon would be, the gentleman was without his blue and yellow handcart. Usually he would be pushing it in front of him, its uneven wheels clinking along the gravel. But the handcart had been confiscated, along with the fruits and green vegetables the man usually sold. So because he had no handcart and no produce, he did not sing his usual song of 'Callaloo! Fresh Callaloo! Ugli fruit and sweet, sweet oranges!' He was a man without his usual context, and therefore had become strange and unfamiliar. No one wanted to meet his gaze. No one wanted to look at him for very long, though they stole quick glances as he walked by.

The man finally turned into the yard where his house was. It was a small yard and an even smaller house – an assemblage of disused timber. The house, like his handcart, was blue and yellow and when the handcart was parked in front, it had a way of blending in, or looking like an extra room that had been added on. In fact, the handcart and the house were not of drastically different sizes. The man opened his door on its rickety latch and then closed it. It made a small clicking sound, which was startling for its quietness. Everyone would have preferred him to slam it.

Now that he was finally inside, everyone could look up, but if they found themselves by accident looking into someone else's eyes, they would turn away as if ashamed and they would try to swallow the large thing that had formed in their throat. They would look down once more at the grass, and the cracks, and the shadows, and the shape of their feet.

They tried not to think about the man, but he was all they thought about that day. And the day after. And then the day after that. In fact, years later, every now and then, people who had witnessed this walk would think about the man, just as Ma Taffy is thinking about him now.

When he had moved into Augustown he had introduced himself as Clarky. The name was accepted without question, and no one knew for sure whether his first name was actually Clark, or maybe his surname was Clarkson, or maybe as a teenager visiting town (he was originally from Westmoreland, he said), he had snuck into the Carib Theatre several times, watched *Gone With the Wind* and had adopted several mannerisms of Clark Gable, thereby earning himself the nickname.

On the evening of the day that Clarky walked into Augustown without his handcart, Ma Taffy had said to her friend, Sister Gilzene, 'So Clarky come back.'

'Mmm-hm,' Sister Gilzene had confirmed.

Ma Taffy's three nieces were playing in the road. They took turns steering a circle of hose with a wire hanger they had straightened out for the purpose of their game. It was a boy's game, and the slight turn of Sister Gilzene's lips made it clear that she disapproved of them playing it, and disapproved more generally of the way Ma Taffy was allowing them to run up and down the street, and sometimes disappear around the corner.

'I guess them never have nothing to keep him in jail for,' Sister Gilzene finally added.

'If they never have nothing to keep him for, then they shoulda never did hold him in the first place.'

Sister Gilzene shrugged. 'Taffy, you know how these police boys stay. I imagine them did just want to rough him up a little. And they think that every Rastaman with a cartful of callaloo really selling ganja.'

'But look how they send him back, Gilly. Look how they make the poor man walk back to his house without . . .'

'Yes yes yes, I know,' Sister Gilzene broke in quickly, 'without his handcart.' In this way she made it clear what still could not be mentioned.

Ma Taffy opened her mouth but closed it again. 'Without his handcart,' she agreed. So they would not talk about Clarky's impressive mane of dreadlocks which had been shaven from his head. It was as if Sister Gilzene, like all of Augustown, shared a little in the man's shame and did not know how to face it, how to give it words.

Clarky had walked back into town without his handcart and without his dreadlocks. Instead, he carried with him this oozing, thick, grey thing. A feeling.

Ma Taffy and Sister Gilzene looked away from each other and up to the sky, which was turning purple. There was a sound in the distance. A kind of commotion.

'What was that?'

'What was what?' Sister Gilzene frowned. Her hearing was not good. But the sound came again and this time she heard it. The girls who had disappeared up the road were squealing.

Ma Taffy stood up as the three girls came running back to the house. They no longer had the circle of hose nor the wire hanger.

Ma Taffy suspected the Wilson brothers immediately. They were always troubling the girls and taking things from them. *A backbone*, she thought. *I must make sure these girls have a strong backbone.* The girls kept squealing all the way back towards the two women.

'All right! All right! Ooonoo, hush up the cowbawling!'

33

Sister Gilzene snapped, for in Augustown any woman could assume the disciplinarian role of mother. But the girls ran straight to Ma Taffy. Six hands grabbed her dress and pinched her and demanded that she come.

'Wait, wait, wait! What all of this for?'

The three girls spoke at once. Little could be discerned from the cacophonous sound, so Ma Taffy focused on Gina, who, although the youngest, was the most articulate. The three-year-old looked up with large wet eyes. 'Come, Aunt Taffy,' she demanded.

Ma Taffy and Sister Gilzene exchanged glances. They rose and followed the girls. They walked up the road, the dust speckling their feet. They came to the blue and yellow house. The girls dashed around the side of the house towards the backyard. The women followed but it was a squeeze, for the space between the shack and the wall was tiny.

In the backyard they now saw the gentleman standing under a large Julie mango tree. His face was slumped onto his chest as if in prayer. It was hard to look on his bald dome.

Ma Taffy looked down, and it was then that she saw the space between Clarky's feet and the ground. He wasn't standing at all. He was floating. The rope round his neck attached him like a pendant to the thickest branch of the mango tree.

Ma Taffy could hear Sister Gilzene's hollow refrain of, 'Saschrise! Saschrise! Jeezas Chrise!' She could hear the three girls sniffling, but the sound seemed far away. One by one the three girls tried to hug Ma Taffy, but she shrugged each one of them off. Her eyes focused on those few inches between Clarky and the ground, the blades of grass that seemed, even then, to be trying to reach up to his bare feet as if they could still rescue him. Ma Taffy wondered if she could just scoop up a bit of ground and bring it to Clarky's feet, if that might make him catch another breath – cough himself back into life. She could not look up at his legs, or his torso, or at the rope that seemed mockingly to resemble a thick dreadlock. But most of all, she could not look on his shining bald head.

And Ma Taffy wondered why they made it mean so much, this Nazirite vow she herself had taken: *No blade shall ever touch my head.* It was just hair, after all. It was just hair. It could grow back. It was nothing for a big, big man to lose his life over. But in her heart, Ma Taffy knew it was more than enough to die for. She knew that for people to be people, they had to believe in something. They had to believe that something was worth believing in. And they had to carry that thing in their hearts and guard it, for once you believed in something, in anything at all, Babylon would try its damnedest to find out what that thing was, and they would try to take it from you.

Even so, Ma Taffy now finds herself holding onto Kaia's knees and repeating this very lie to him again and again: 'Is only hair, my boy. Is only hair. It will grow back. It is only hair. You understand me?'

'Yes, Grandma,' the boy nods.

'But you have to do something for me, Kaia, and do it quick, quick. Go down the river to 'Gola and call Soft-Paw. Tell him to make haste and come. Tell him that Ma Taffy need to see him now.'

4

There are duffel bags of guns underneath the house, concealed in a mound of sand. Ma Taffy knows that they are there. She feels their sinister presence, how the bags just squat there like terrible frogs, pulsing their dark and inscrutable hearts. Sometimes she believes she even smells them – their metallic ugliness, and the traces of sulphur after they have been used. The bags have changed the balance of things so much that Ma Taffy does not like their presence.

The artillery belongs to the boys of the Angola Gang. They have not asked permission to hide their guns and ammunition under the house, and in fact, Ma Taffy isn't even sure that the whole gang knows of this location. In fact, the more she thinks about it, the more she doubts it. If they knew, there would have been more traffic passing through her yard at night, but only Soft-Paw ever comes through. She understands then that his leadership of the gang depends on this secret knowledge. It is his stash; the guns are for him to distribute, to dole out like rewards, but always with the understanding that they ultimately belong to him. This secret under Ma Taffy's house is the source of his power.

The police once came into Augustown for a major operation – a whole truckload of them, with dogs and backup from the Army. They combed the riverbed near 'Gola, turning over every stone, digging up the sand. They found three, maybe four guns, and the next day it was all over the newspapers. Major Haul Of Weapons Found In Augustown. For a mere four guns. There are many times more guns than that under Ma Taffy's house.

She has to give Soft-Paw credit, though, for when he walks into the yard at night he, as usual, never makes a sound. It is as if the earth – every blade of grass, every stone – adjusts itself to make space for him, for the specific shape of his body, so that he walks without ever disturbing things. But if his feet never shift things on the ground, his presence shifts something in the air, and Ma Taffy always knows when he is around.

Usually she says nothing. Even if she is sitting out there, she allows him to come and go, allows him to feel secure in the knowledge that his movements are unknown. But one night, as he was stepping out of the yard, she stopped him.

'How the night treating you, Marlon?'

His foot came down suddenly, hard on the ground, and she could hear him gulping quick breaths. He soon found his balance again.

'Mi awrite, Ma Taffy,' he said to her, and leaned himself against her verandah.

'I don't like none of this, you know,' Ma Taffy said to him.

'We don't have no choice. Dem take Augustown people fi coward. Dem take we as weak. We will show them.'

'But it make me scared. All this warring.'

She could sense the wide grin on Soft-Paw's face. She imagined his white teeth against the night.

'You don't have nothing to be scared bout, Ma Taffy. No harm not coming your way.'

'Who said is me I scared for?'

She felt his grin widen. It was always like that with these rudeboys. They needed a woman – a mother, a grandmother, a girlfriend – to worry over them. They were soldiers, and something about this kind of love sustained them. But the love also reminded Soft-Paw that he was this kind of a soldier, and that he was involved in a war, and so the grin went away quickly. His face became the mask he had now been practising for a while. He spat on the floor.

'Scared for what, Ma Taffy? That them kill me? Yes. They might kill me. Plenty people waah fi see me dead. Even people here in Augustown. And it will happen. Today. Tomorrow. But what in that? Better you dead strong, like a warrior, than you live you whole life bend-over and taking pure kick up from Babylon.'

If she had been another kind of a woman she might have said to him, *But you are a smart young man. You have your whole life ahead of you. You still can make something of yourself.* But she did not believe such things. What was a whole life, after all, and was it always worth it? She knew that there were other people in this world – young people – who had never seen another young person die. They thought death only came to their grandparents, who lived in retirement homes, and who, upon dying, gathered the family around them and left them money in their will. Such young people lived their youth never thinking about the inevitability of their own death. That was a special kind of luxury, and it was one which she knew Soft-Paw would never have, so she was silent.

There was a gunshot in the distance, and Ma Taffy could

feel Soft-Paw's body become tense again. 'Goodnight, Marlon,' she said to him.

He nodded and slipped back into the night.

When they gather, one on top of the other, and roll in waves from house to house along a street or a lane, whispers have a way of sounding like the wind; and so, as Soft-Paw walks with Kaia up from the river, through the zinc lanes and towards Ma Taffy's house, his arms around the boy's shoulders like a father, it sounds as though a light breeze is following them. It takes a moment and a squinting of the eyes, but by and by the people recognise Kaia. But wait! they whisper, *That's the Rasta pickney, nuh true? Yes, is him. He got a funny name, I can't remember, but is him for true. And he live with the two Rasta ladies — the old woman and her niece.* Then another whisper rolls on top of the first — *I hear something happen at the school. Some teacherman take up his scissors and cut off the boy's hair! Woiiii! You believe such a thing?! Cut off the lickle Rasta yute hair just so!*

Now here he is, walking up the street with Soft-Paw. *Is him who they call Soft-Paw? Yes! That's him. Eh-eh! I think him was a big, big man — but him is just a yute himself! Missis, don't watch that. Him is the baddest bad man in this area. Is him lead the Angola Gang. He call himself the Defender of Augustown.*

One little girl who goes by the name of Lloydisha cannot contain her excitement as she hears the whispers all about her. She runs around her yard snapping her fingers and singing loudly, 'Yes now! Spanish Town!' She stretches this word 'Spanish' out into 'Spaaanish'. It is the chorus Jamaican children sing whenever trouble is coming — Spanish Town being where the gallows were. They do not always know the meaning of the song. They do not know about the gallows.

And yet they sing it, 'Yes now! Spaaanish Town!'

Soft-Paw reaches Ma Taffy's house and climbs the steps up to her verandah.

'Ma Taffy,' Soft-Paw says gallantly, delivering the boy back to his grandmother. Kaia settles back onto the seat beside the old woman.

'Thank you for coming. I hope I never disturb you from nothing too important.'

'Anyting happen in Augustown is important to me, Ma Taffy. And anybody trouble you or your family, well they fuck with the wrong people. Whoever did do this wickedness to the lickle yute, don't worry. I will make sure him get deal with proper! Just say the word.'

Ma Taffy is silent for almost an entire minute. Soft-Paw waits, but she says no word at all. At last she sighs as if she has been holding her breath. 'Soft-Paw,' she begins, and the rudeboy stands up even straighter because it is the first time Ma Taffy has called him by that name. She is addressing him now not as a little boy, Marlon, but as a big man – as the leader of a gang. 'The teacherman who did do this will get dealt with. But that fight is not your fight.'

Soft-Paw is confused. 'Then why you call . . .'

'Because I need you to take away the guns. Today. Right now. You have to move them.'

Soft-Paw opens his eyes wide and then frowns, and something shifts in the air between the young man and the old woman, a kind of menace. Ma Taffy had feared this, for she is not asking a favour of him, which is what he would have liked. He is the kind of man desperate to offer his patronage to as many people as ask, so that they will be in his debt. Instead Ma Taffy is demanding something of him, and

40

something he does not want to do. She knows that Soft-Paw respects her, but he is also young and with more power than he ought to have, and that makes him dangerous. How can she now explain to him things she only half knows herself – things she only feels – a smell of something coming? But the guns cannot stay. She knows that much. Even more dangerous than a rudeboy with a gun and a gang is an overprotective mother with a deep anger inside her. Gina will come home soon enough. She will find her son without the dreadlocks she has made him grow since birth, and something is bound to explode. It does not take much to provoke Gina on the best of days. She has already been through so much. And this surely is the worst of days. Ma Taffy knows that when a hurricane is coming, you make sure to cut the heaviest branches off of nearby trees, for the hurricane is already dangerous all on its own and you don't want to supply it with additional weapons. The logic is the same now. Something is coming, and the temptation of guns and bullets nearby is not sensible.

'Look,' Ma Taffy says. 'Things and things is going to happen today, and I can't tell you more than that. But I don't want no guns here today, and I feel you won't want them here neither. Not if you know what I know. Trust me. Babylon might come here tonight. You don't want no guns here.'

Soft-Paw grits his teeth. This blasted-know-too-much-fi-her-own-damn-good woman, he is thinking. There isn't even any point in denying the fact of the guns he keeps underneath her house. Obviously she has never seen them, and he is sure that she has never disturbed the spot where they are, yet somehow she knows. And he remembers now the night that they spoke about it, though without ever saying

41

so. 'I don't like none of this,' she had told him, and he had walked away wondering how much she really did know – how specific or how general were these things she did not like. He respects Ma Taffy; this is true. Her knowing has helped him before. It helped him to kill that eedyat police bwoy. He owes her for that. But he sees himself as helping to build a new Augustown, and in this new dispensation of the place, it is possible for a man or a woman to know too much. In this Augustown, man could dead for knowing the wrong things. This old woman, he thinks, belongs to another time and place. She belongs to an Augustown that he has only heard talk about – the one that was once just a country hamlet, a simple village.

Soft-Paw does not know the precise changes that have taken place, and yet he too has been a part of them.

As Jamaica settled itself into the twentieth century, Kingston began to spread from its harbour, rippling out into the dormitory parish of St Andrew that surrounded it. The ebbless wave of the city frothed its way up towards Half Way Tree, then further up Hope Road towards Liguanea, Mona, Papine and, inevitably, Augustown. To its own surprise, the village found that it was no longer five miles away from the city, but on its edge and then comfortably inside it. Kingston flooded in. Houses were connected to the water main of the NWC and to the electric grid of JPS. The residents of Augustown, new urbanites as they were, now, no longer tolerated the countrified designation of 'village'. Instead, they spoke of themselves as living in a Kingston community. But no sooner had the village graduated to 'community' than its middle-class neighbours made sure to distinguish themselves with the prefix 'suburban' and Augustown with the prefix, 'inner city'. Like dark magic, that phrase seemed to draw into Augustown a heaviness and a heat and a rot. Rusting zinc fences now line the streets, and ratchet knives and machine guns have appeared in the hands of young men. A scar now defaces the overlooking hillside.

Soft-Paw is therefore part and parcel of this new Augustown, and he knows enough of its past to think that soon this place will no longer have space for little old women like Ma Taffy, women with this higher science and obeah knowledge. This new Augustown will deal in bullets, because bullet is stronger than obeah. Bullet is stronger than Anancy stories and all that old-time wisdom. So this old woman had better learn how to mind herself!

'I will move them,' he says finally, 'but I can't move them now. Is broad daylight. Too much eyes will . . .'

'Please, Soft-Paw.' Her lips are trembling. She does this on purpose. 'You have to move them now. I wouldn't call you here otherwise. You is becoming a powerful man, and I is just an old woman getting weaker and weaker every day. I never ask you no favour before. I asking you this one.'

He is silent. So the old woman will be in his debt after all. This appeases him. After a moment he goes over and puts his arms around her shoulders the way he had had his arms around Kaia's, as if he were her father and protector.

'Awrite, old woman,' he says, purposely not using her name, at once ascribing her with age and yet infantilising her. 'Don't you worry your little head. Soft-Paw will move the guns fi you.'

And it is one of the things Augustown will remember about this day: how the gunman, Soft-Paw, had walked back down the lane lugging two rucksacks, how the shapes of handguns and machine rifles were clear through the canvas of those two bags, and how they had all caught their breath upon seeing this. The guns were in the bags but people still squinted at the shininess of them, and it felt afterwards that the shape of those guns became the shape of the entire day.

5

Long after the last school bell has rung, Mr Emanuel Saint-Josephs sits in the musty classroom of 2B as if rooted to his desk. Every ten minutes or so he feels the urge to get up and go home, but this is followed by an intense terror washing over his whole body. Beads of sweat gather like a sprinkle of morning dew on his forehead and he has to settle right back into his seat. He knows that this terror is connected to the thing he did earlier, so instinctively he goes over the whole drama in as much detail as he can remember. It is therefore not the incident itself that is tiring, but this constant reliving of it, and his absolute inability to leave the scene. It is as if he is waiting on a repercussion the shape of which he cannot yet discern.

His reliving of the event begins with the moment when he turned his back to the class. He had been writing out the two times table on the blackboard. He drew big and beautiful numbers. Blue chalk dust drifted down onto his arms and into his nose. He made snorting sounds as he tried not to sneeze. Imagining the children would be making a face at this, he turned round suddenly to keep them in order. He glared at them and they grinned back at him. To the children, this sudden turning around by their teacher was something like a game of peekaboo. Mr Saint-Josephs grimaced and returned to the blackboard. He was a somewhat nervous man, and did not like having his back to the class. It made him feel exposed and vulnerable. It was a large class for just the one teacher. There were three rows of tables across, and four back. Each desk seated two children. The walls of the classroom had been made with decorative blocks that someone probably thought would have let light in through the patterns, but this was not the case. It was a very dark classroom, the only illumination coming from the two long-tubed fluorescent lights overhead.

Mr Saint-Josephs heard the distinct sound of giggling, and turned around again just in time to catch the Rastafari boy, Kaia McDonald, whispering into the ear of the other little boy who sat beside him. *The nerve!* the teacher thought to himself. *The outright nerve!*

Many hours later, he keeps on saying this in his head, *The nerve! The nerve!* working himself up into a frenzy, pretending that the misdemeanour wasn't in fact as small and common as it in fact was.

He has been expecting the principal to come storming in, but it seems certain now that Kaia has not actually gone to Mrs Garrick's office but instead has cried his way home. Mr Saint-Josephs imagines that he would have been ready to face the principal anyway. He had rehearsed a little speech in his mind. 'The boy was acting like a living hooligan, ma'am! A living hooligan, I say! And what else to expect? If we allow these little boys and girls to . . . well . . . to look and dress like any madman or madwoman walking on the road – no little tidiness bout them, no little grooming, no little hygiene – then what else to expect? I had to take matters in hand,

Mrs G! And I warn you bout this already. On my very first day, I come to your office and warn you.'

And this was true. On his first day of teaching he had barged into the principal's office. 'Look here, Miss Garrick,' he had begun at once, 'I expect my students to be properly put together. And tidy! Yes, they must be tidy. We cannot be asking any less of these young gentlemen and -women at such a crucial and impressionable age!'

Mrs G had looked up, unable to hide the annoyance in her eyes. She took off her glasses slowly and put down the pen she had been writing reports with, then she fixed the teacher with a withering look. 'Good morning, Mr Saint-Josephs. What is this about?'

Mr Saint-Josephs had stuttered, 'Miss Garrick . . .'

'Mrs Garrick,' she corrected him.

Mr Saint-Josephs sighed and rolled his eyes. 'Mrs Garrick,' he said with great affectation, 'I am here this morning in front of you to talk about the matter of decorum and good manners and tidiness which it look to me like the students here don't have! When I was Deputy Head Teacher in a very upstanding school in Trelawny, we made—'

'Mr Saint-Josephs,' she said, cutting him off, 'we have very high standards here at Augustown Primary, and we do expect you, as a teacher, to uphold these standards. Students must always, ALWAYS, be in proper uniform. Girls in their blue tunics with white shirts, and boys in their khakis with their shirts tucked in, and with a black or brown belt.'

'Miss Garrick,' he boomed, 'there is right this very minute a little boy sitting down in my classroom, and it don't even look to me like he come to school to learn. It look to me like he come to school to sell brooms.'

'I'm sorry, I'm not catching your meaning.'

'Dreadlocks, Miss Garrick! *Dreadlocks!* Like some dirty little African from the bush, and sitting right there in front of me, so brazen with his hairstyle. No, no, no! I will not tolerate it. When I was Deputy Head Teacher at—'

'What is the child's name?' Mrs Garrick had asked.

'Ma'am. I never even stop to ask the boy's name. I take one look at him and my blood pressure boil up so high that I come straight to your office.'

The principal placed her spectacles back on her face and lifted her pen. She did not even look up at Mr Saint-Josephs as she said, quite curtly, 'I believe he is a Rastafari child, Mr Saint-Josephs. Good day.'

'B-b-but I was made to understand when I accept this job — stepping down, you might remember, from my previous position of Deputy Head Teacher — that this was going to be a Christian school.'

Still looking down at her work, and beginning to fill in the overdue reports, Mrs Garrick said, once again, though even more slowly and sharply, 'Mr Saint-Josephs. Good day!'

So Mr Saint-Josephs had turned on his heel and stormed out of the office more angry than when he had come in. He shut the door of Mrs G's office with exactly enough force to signal his anger but not enough for it to be considered a slam.

So now today, as he sits in the classroom, he remembers this, and thinks it is partly the principal's fault because she does not have good standards and did nothing about the situation when he raised it. But the principal has not turned up, and Mr Saint-Josephs is put out, perhaps in the way that a man who has battened up his house for a hurricane and has bought candles and a month's worth of tinned food is secretly disappointed when the storm passes without causing damage.

'No, no. I can't stay here no more. I going. I going home.' Mr Saint-Josephs says this aloud and starts to stand up, but once again the terror washes over him. He falls back into the chair and looks at his fingers. He flexes them open and closed, open and closed, and then pushes them underneath his buttocks as if sitting on them will make them feel less guilty.

'Why you don't stop talking and misbehaving in class, eh! Why you don't stop talking?!' This is what he had shouted in Kaia's face. And he can still feel the small weight of that little boy as he had pulled him by his dreadlocks out of his chair – so surprisingly light. He felt he could have lifted the boy right up into the air. But even more surprising was the release of that weight, like a small pop, when he took the pair of rusty scissors and barbered the boy. He had not planned on doing such a thing. The idea had come into his head suddenly, like an inspiration, and then the deed had been done. It had surprised him how the clump of dread-locks was suddenly in his hands like a slither of snakes.

The class went silent. Mr Saint-Josephs did not know that six-year-olds could hold their breath like that. Their eyes bulged as Kaia reached his small hands up to his head. When his hands came down onto jagged bits of hair and raw scalp – his own head suddenly made foreign to him – his eyes flooded, though no sound came out of his mouth as yet.

'You think I give you nothing to cry bout yet! Eh? You think I give you nothing to cry bout?' Mr Saint-Josephs was affecting the supercilious tone of an adult reproaching a naughty child, but in the middle of his voice there was the trace of an emotion the children were not used to hearing in an adult: he was afraid. They were being ushered into a new understanding of the world – one in which adults were not always right. They were aware, also, of their own power in this moment, but only in a vague way, and they did not know what to do about it. Instinctively they wanted to flash their hands and sing out, 'Yesss now, Spaaanish Town!' But who had ever sung such a song to a fully grown adult? It was a peculiar position to be in.

Mr Saint-Josephs knew he had to do something quickly. He had to regain control. He turned to Kaia and shouted, 'Get out of my classroom right now. Get out!'

Kaia turned and seemed to wobble out of classroom 2B.

Mr Saint-Josephs focused on the rest of the class. 'Two times two is?'

They did not respond.

'TWO TIMES TWO IS . . .?'

The children looked at each other, confused.

'Then what happen?!' Mr Saint-Josephs chided. 'I teaching a set of dunce pickney? Eh? All of you dunce, or what? You don't know what two times two is? Come, man! TWO TIMES TWO IS?'

It was a chant pulling them back towards him, and it worked. The students sitting near the front of the class lost their resolve and finally muttered the answer, 'Four.' The children sitting right behind, not wanting to be left out, caught on and muttered it as well; and so this muttering of 'four' stretched out like a wave, from the front of the class to the back.

Mr Saint-Josephs slammed his fist on the table and bellowed

a last time: 'I SAID TWO TIMES TWO ISSSS?' It was so loud even the classes nearby heard and wanted to answer. His entire class now shouted in unison, 'FOUR!'

Every lesson for the last hour of the day was taught in this almost Pentecostal fashion. Circles of damp spread from his underarms as Mr Saint-Josephs shouted and flailed, making sure to keep everyone's attention.

But the day is done now. The students have gone home and he is still sitting in the classroom, reliving the moment he has been trying to avoid. The pair of scissors is now lying innocently beside the cookie tin in which he keeps his blackboard duster and chalks. The dreadlocks are scattered on the floor. An occasional breeze brings them to life so that they really do look like snakes.

Mr Saint-Josephs wonders, with an insight that is not common to him, if his world is falling apart. He wonders if, despite all his attempts to bring the same strict order to his life as he had had in Trelawny, things are not still unravelling – if he is not becoming undone.

6

The strange and fastidious ways of Mr Saint-Josephs have followed him all the way from his two-bedroom country house in Trelawny to the single room he now rents in the backyard of a Mona bungalow. He continues to wake up at fifteen minutes to five each morning, then stay under the sheets until the clock actually strikes five, trying to resist the urge to take himself into his own hands and masturbate. At five a.m. he will light the flame of his tilley lamp and, by its warm light, read exactly two pages of the Bible followed by two pages of Charles Darwin's On the Origin of Species. That the two books contradict each other is not a thought that ever occurs to him. He understands very little of either text, but he is still making his way, slowly and carefully, through both, imagining that with each sentence read he has improved himself in some profound way.

After his morning reading he will say a prayer – the long and earnest kind usually uttered by old women – and it is the kind of affectation which, from the lips of a young man, can never actually be sanctioned as 'effeminate', since it exists in the realm of the spiritual, but which nonetheless makes the grandfathers and uncles of such boys feel just a little uncomfortable. It is the sort of prayer never contained in the closet of one's mind but one that spills out through the corners of ever-moving lips, and that is accompanied by 'hallelujahs' and occasional sharp twitches.

After his prayer, Mr Saint-Josephs will go to the bathroom, where a kerosene tin filled with water is waiting. He bathes carefully and efficiently, using no more than the one kerosene tin. The water is always cold and biting, having been collected the night before.

But the kerosene tin with its cold water and the tilley lamp with its flickering flame are unnecessary. Mr Saint-Josephs has brought them with him from Trelawny and there is no need for them now that he is living in the city. There is electric light in his room and hot running water in the bathroom, yet Mr Saint-Josephs insists on keeping to his rural ways, imagining that the use of too many modern luxuries will lead to comfort, and that comfort will in turn lead to the weakening of his moral fortitude.

Mr Saint-Josephs, after his bath, will observe himself in the mirror. He is always pleased to see a man fair of complexion, with a strong jaw and soft curly hair that betrays a kind of mixed-race heritage that is typical on islands like Jamaica. But if Mr Saint-Josephs observes such things with pleasure, and indeed pride, he also observes them with a great deal of imagination and fantasy. To everyone else, he is a man dark of complexion; his round face evidences no jawline whatsoever and his extremely thick hair reveals that, if he is mixed with anything, it is with Ashanti and Yoruba. He is not an unattractive man, and yet he carries himself in an unattractive way. So strong and so desperate is his belief that he is other than what he actually is, that he moves his body in awkward ways, squeezes it into the wrong clothes,

53

gives it gestures and mannerisms and styles that he probably imagines are graceful but which come across as clumsy and buffoonish. Take, for instance, the way he will vigorously oil and comb and brush his hair each morning, over to the left, over to the right, over to the left, over to the right, until he has formed the sharpest, neatest parting in the middle of his head. Well, as soon as he steps away from the mirror, patches of it will spring back up, his hair trying desperately to re-form itself into its natural afro, and so by the time Mr Saint-Josephs has got to work, his hair always resembles an unevenly cut field, which in turn has earned him the nick-name 'Pitchy-Patchy-Head'.

Mr Saint-Josephs, to put it simply, suffers from a deeply incorrect notion of things, and the only person who ever dared to tell him the truth (because it had become blindingly obvious to her one afternoon as she hid her vagina from his gaze) was his wife. In return for this small nugget of truth, the truth-teller received a broken nose.

The brown-haired Mary Bridgelong met her future ex-husband when she had come to that age at which young girls, in order to assert themselves as independent and free-thinking, lose faith in just about everything associated with their upbringing. It is that season in which the religious become agnostics; the meat-eaters become vegetarians; and the fair-skinned and privileged of Jamaica (the class to which Mary Bridgelong belonged) become placard-bearing supporters of black power. For most girls it is only a season. It passes. Important decisions must not be made during its short length; but no one could convince Mary of this. It was the 1970s, and so the nineteen-year-old had decided to lose faith in the fair-skinned, straight-haired world of her family who, not by virtue of their wealth (which was hardly substantial), but by what in Jamaica would be called their 'brownness', were considered part of the petit bourgeoisie of Trelawny.

Mary was not pretty, but she was indeed brown, and in Jamaica this counted for something. There were many eligible brown men she could have married. She could have had brown babies, and established herself forever in a class slightly above the black majority. As for her choice among blackmen, that was almost limitless. It was curious, then, that Mary decided to take a fancy to the Deputy Head Teacher of the Basic School – Mr Emanuel Saint-Josephs – who every morning and every evening walked by her gate towards the school where he worked. Perhaps it was simply that, heavy-set as he was, and with such a magnificent moustache, Mr Saint-Josephs reminded her a little of Marcus Garvey, whose writings she had begun to read.

She found excuses to be out at the gate in the mornings when he walked by, and also in the evenings. They nodded hello to each other, but she found it hard to pull him into a deeper conversation. She began to help out at the school, started walking with Mr Saint-Josephs to the campus and then back home to her gate in the evenings. Around him she became her most flirtatious self. She found excuses to touch him on his knee, or to fix his hair. Yet he showed no signs that the attraction was mutual.

This man, Mary had thought even then, is as dead to me as stone!

This should have been a sign to her. Still, she was only nineteen, and more than a little foolish, and so Mr Saint-Josephs' complete non-reciprocation only made her infatuation grow to unhealthy proportions.

One evening as they walked home together from the Basic School, the air smelling of June plums and scotch bonnet pepper, a radio in the distance playing a Justin Hinds tune, Mary had felt moved to turn around to the Deputy Head Teacher and kiss him on the lips. 'Mr Saint-Josephs,' she said to him as she withdrew her wet lips from his, 'let us get married. I've been thinking about it for a while. I suppose you have as well.' She said this last bit hesitantly. She looked up and then away from what seemed to be his stricken face. But she continued, before she lost her nerve, 'There really is nothing to stop us. So, what do you say?'

Just like that. A full proposal, and not just for a date, but for marriage. Mary had decided she was in love, and perhaps she was. But it was with everything else: the 1970s, black power, dashikis, afros. She was in love with being young and having possibilities. She imagined that in the person of Mr Saint-Josephs she would be marrying into the new black elite of the island.

To the stunned Mr Saint-Josephs, Mary's proposal was proof of something he had always suspected about himself: his own fairness of skin, his own softness of hair, his own mixed-race gentility. Marriage to her would be an exaltation, at last, out of the blackness to which some unobservant people thought he belonged. He was trembling when he said, 'Yes, Miss Bridgelong. Yes, of course we should get married!' as if the idea had always been in his head.

After a few weeks of marriage to her future ex-husband, Mary could not help but notice the man's reluctance to have sex with her. After two years they had done the deed a total of seven and a quarter times. (She counted as a mere quarter the night when she had virtually raped him. She had straddled his limp penis and began gyrating before he finally threw her off, saying, 'Goddammit, Mary. I too tired tonight!' Then he had rolled his large body over, turning himself away from her, trembling.) It hurt Mary when she realised that Mr Saint-Josephs had no problem actually getting his manhood up. There were mornings when she, pretending to be still asleep, became aware of him – his eyes squeezed shut – masturbating right there beside her in the bed. After he came, he would sigh deeply, wipe the semen off of his stomach and smear it against the wall. He would get out of bed then, light the tilley lamp and begin to read his Bible.

When she was twenty-one, Mary Saint-Josephs, nee Bridge-long, accepted that she had made a mistake. She decided as well that she was still young and still brown and could still have almost any man she wanted, and some of those men were still giving her signals. She accepted that in the near future she would almost certainly divorce Mr Saint-Josephs, but she wouldn't rush into another marriage. No. She was wiser now. She would have to test-drive the merchandise.

Mary soon developed a whole schedule whereby a few different men would visit her during the day at the two-bedroom house in Trelawny while Mr Saint-Josephs was out teaching at the Basic School. In the end, it only surprised Mary that the man took so long to catch her in the act.

Mr Saint-Josephs had come home early that afternoon and noticed a blue VW parked underneath a Julie mango tree outside his house. He noticed that a soft mango had fallen and burst on top of the car roof, and that flies were buzzing around the spilt orange flesh. He observed the flies for a moment, and then the car, and thought to himself that he had never seen it before. On the basis of such vehicular proof, other men in his position would have put two and two together. They would each have known the truth of their wife's infidelity right then because, on a certain level, they had known it all along – from the moment the wives had stopped nagging them for sex and had begun strutting around with the languid elegance that is only achieved when a woman has grown used to being thoroughly satisfied in bed. But Mr Saint-Josephs simply shrugged and walked towards the house.

He let himself in and approached the bedroom, where the door was shut. Then he heard the muffled and deeply satisfied groans of his wife. These were sounds he had never been able to draw out of her in the seven and a quarter times they had done the deed. At last he understood what was happening. He eased the bedroom door open.

At first the couple did not notice him. Mr Saint-Josephs observed the distinctly fair buttocks of a young man thrusting in and out of Mary's spread legs. He cleared his throat. The couple still did not hear or notice him.

'You slut!' Mr Saint-Josephs growled.

Even to his own ears this sounded pathetic. It was a sound made without conviction, as if, much like his clothes, he was trying on something else that didn't quite fit. But the pathetic sound at least did the job of announcing his presence. The couple scrambled in impossible directions, the man first crawling towards the bedpost, therefore pushing himself even deeper into Mary, who grunted even more deeply, before pulling himself out completely, accompanied by the wet slap of his cock against his torso. He stood up, and Mr Saint-Josephs tried to avert his eyes from the pink erection waving itself in front of him. The young man held his hands above his head.

'I'm . . . I'm sorry, sir. Please be calm!'

He was lean and tall. The hair all over his body was slicked down with sweat. He scraped his clothes from the floor and used them to cover his finally deflating erection.

As yet, Mary had said nothing. She had only drawn the sheets up to cover her lower parts.

'I'm so sorry, I'm so sorry!' the man continued, turning from Mary to Mr Saint-Josephs, unsure as to who deserved his apology more. He hurried out of the room. The front door of the house slammed, an engine started, then it grew faint as it headed off into the distance.

Mary looked down at the sheets. Mr Saint-Josephs glared.

'Slut!' he said again, and this time managed it with more conviction and so tried one better: 'Raasclawt slut.' But he was not used to cursing, and the words sounded forced on his tongue. Mary finally looked up, and this caused Mr Saint-Josephs to stumble backwards. He had expected to see embarrassment, even contrition in those eyes. He had been readying himself to exploit it – to use it as leverage in the new power he imagined himself holding. But the brown-haired Mary was looking at him with pity.

'You stupid man.' She said it without any hint of malice. Indeed, she said it in a surprised sort of a way, as one might when struck by a truth that has managed to escape one's notice for years. Mary gasped, and then spoke the truth again, dumbstruck by the obviousness of it all. 'You *are* a very stupid man. Oh, lord. That's it. You are just a very stupid man.'

She had believed so much in the politics of the 1970s,

in black power, in the redress of old white wrongs, and she had read so much of Marcus Garvey, that it had never occurred to her that a man such as Emanuel Saint-Josephs, heavyset and with such a magnificent moustache, could possibly have been stupid. She saw now that just because history had wronged gentlemen such as him, and to precisely that extent had also ennobled them, it did not follow that they were all equally enlightened. She understood too that the failure of her marriage was more her fault than his – that a man as stupid as he was couldn't really be blamed. It was she who had made a fetish out of him.

Mary looked up again at this man who was now both strange and understandable to her. 'I'm sorry, Mr Saint-Josephs,' she said. 'It's just that you really are a very stupid blackman.'

Ironic, really, that it was in this moment that Mary had come the closest to truly being married to Mr Saint-Josephs, for it was with the instinctiveness of a long-wedded spouse that she had finally found his trigger. To be called 'stupid' was one thing. To be called 'black' was quite another. He could not accept this callous demotion back into what he imagined he had been exalted out of. And that it had been sincerely meant, and was therefore possibly true, was enough to begin his unravelling.

Mary had turned to look out of the window. She heard, just in time, the beastly grunt. She turned back to find her future ex-husband lunging towards her. He hit her with a closed fist. Her nose flattened under the weight of the impact. The nose sagged at an odd angle. Mary cried out as she held her nose in place. Mr Saint-Josephs was breathing heavily over her, feeling as close to tears as he had ever felt.

Mary, inexplicably, felt the need to comfort him, but she didn't.

'Mary . . . you betray me . . . in the worst way . . . today,' Mr Saint-Josephs said when he could finally manage a few words.

'I have,' she said quietly and matter-of-factly.

Mr Saint-Josephs began to make a terrible sound then: dry and scratchy sobs. His eyes became red, even though no water flowed from them. His pain was real, though. He did not understand why, or how, even with a broken nose, Mary could not bring herself to sound contrite or to shed a tear or two herself.

That was almost a year ago, and though Mr Saint-Josephs has not really thought about it again – and certainly won't now as he sits in classroom 2B – the incident has still left a wound, a sense of shame and inadequacy that he will never shake, and with it an ache and a longing he can't quite name. He has left Trelawny. He does not think about the incident, or much about his wife. He is not a contemplative or a reflective man. It is not his habit to ruminate on things. But perhaps the specific wound that Mary left on him is in fact a sense of himself: a self he does not care to know but which he most certainly is.

7

Some days have more roads than others, and some roads more distance, so that when a woman complains how long the day is, maybe she is counting its roads rather than its hours. Ma Taffy is a woman who understands this – the true length of days – and so while Mr Saint-Josephs is in his class-room, rooted to his desk, she is on her verandah walking in a circle. So consistent is this orbital march that it seems to create its own music, her walking stick tap-tap-tapping and her slippered feet pressing the same planks of wood, drawing out of them melody and harmony, a symphony of creaks.

Ma Taffy does not hear the music. She is lost in her thoughts. The guns have been taken away – but what next? What else can she do? She wishes she was the kind of woman who knew other things – the candles to light, the oil to pour, the tea to brew that would create a place of peace. But she does not know such things. She only knows that this day is going to be long – her whole body knows it – and her feet, of their own accord, are trying to find the winding and dangerous road they suspect they will have to walk.

As she goes round and round, Ma Taffy is tilting her head at an angle and observing the boy. It is the angle which she dislikes, the angle from which she is able to glimpse the very little of things that she still can see. The deep dark she is accustomed to has left, and the world has now resolved itself as a silver-blue haze full of shadows. Now she can see silhouettes of trees and houses and people. She can see the boy's shorn head. The sight, dim as it is, makes the old woman swallow hard. What she has suspected is indeed true. This boy she once rescued from a toilet bowl has become smaller. And it isn't just his hair. Something else has been cut out from him – something Ma Taffy suspects will never grow back; something the little boy doesn't even know how to cry for yet.

It occurs to Ma Taffy that whenever Kaia's hair grows back, it will almost certainly grow soft and straight. It will look like white people's hair. For his short life, the boy's dreadlocks have hidden this fact from him. But when Kaia grows his mulatto hair, will he then realise something about himself – something about his father – something that his mother has not bothered to tell him?

It is a question which Ma Taffy herself has never voiced, and yet it lingers between herself and Gina on the skin of their relationship, like a rash.

Ma Taffy forces herself to sit down once more beside the boy, and she picks up the story of the flying preacherman where she left it. 'In them days, the whole place did smell of shit.'

'What?' Kaia is confused. He has forgotten that they are in the middle of a story.

'Augustown,' Ma Taffy explains. 'In those days when the preacherman did begin to float. The whole place did smell of shit. Is just now I remembering it – the smell. Every jackman and -woman from every corner of Jamaica was pouring into

63

Augustown. They just kept on coming – people like ants. Thousands upon thousands of them. You couldn't imagine such a thing if you wasn't there. Some of them was even coming back from foreign – from Panama and Curaçao – all because they hear what was happening and, more importantly, what was going to happen. The ones who come first, well, they get lucky. Maybe they would cotch with people, but before long every house cork and we never have no space to put up nobody else. Some people sleep up at the church, at Union Camp, some put up tent, and some just lay down cardboard on the tough ground outside and when they want to shit or piss, they do it right there, and so after a week the whole place did stink.'

Maas Bilby and Miss Norah's house was one of those that was graced with an early visitor before the real crowds came. That morning, they heard a stone tapping at the door and Maas Bilby looked over at Norah, his brow creased in a question. She shrugged. Maas Bilby lifted himself up, walked over to the door and unfastened it. It swung open and let in the dawn. Little Irene had also risen from her cot, and she walked right behind her stepfather, squeezing herself under his large arms to see who was out there so early.

The little girl recognised the woman standing outside as 'Aunt Mathilda' – a distant relation of her mother. Aunt Mathilda was tall and bony with a nose like a hawk. She was an older woman, but her skin was so tight on her body that you could hardly see her wrinkles. Her head was now wrapped in a green cloth. She wore a long white skirt and a white shirt that looked like it had once been half of a nurse's uniform. Aunt Mathilda and Maas Bilby had never been friendly towards each other. Aunt Mathilda, religious as she was, disapproved of Bilby's petty thieving and thought any relation of hers could have done better. Still, she eventually handed Maas Bilby a small crocus bag.

'Jimbilin and oranges,' she said.

Maas Bilby nodded thank you.

Aunt Mathilda cleared her throat. 'A piece of news reach me all the way in Clarendon, and so I come here special to see if any truth in it.' She looked at Maas Bilby with a curious intensity, as if she were trying to read his brain. 'They saying that another miracle getting ready to take place right here in Augustown. An even more splendocious miracle than that whole business before with the river.'

Mona River had become famous when the preacherman announced it was a healing stream. Although that was over fifteen years ago, Maas Bilby could almost remember the sermon word for word:

'My good people, de word of God has come onto me saying, "Once I made water wine. Behold! Now I make water medicine. And you, Bedward, have I ordained as my Dispenser, Watchman, Shepherd and Trumpeter." Come all ye people and dip inna the healing stream. Get dipped and be healed!'

People were sceptical at first. The water of the Mona River was brown and thick. But it was hard to deny the testimonies that steadily rose out of those waters. Some people went to the river to prove the preacherman wrong – to prove that it was all a hoax – but when even they came out of the waters refreshed and restored from ailments they had almost forgotten they had, they ended up being the loudest converts. The governor and the assembly panicked. They didn't like the atmosphere – hundreds of black people working themselves up into a kind of frenzy. The government sent in their own scientists either to disprove the preacherman or to give a rational explanation for the miracles.

It was the latter – a rational explanation – which they got. The lab reports came back saying that there really were healing minerals in the water. The government published these results in haste, but it only made the preacher's reputation spread even further. For how did he, an unlearned man, know that the dirty Mona River was full of magnesium and zinc and sulphur – words that sounded positively angelic to the peasants? They reckoned he must really have heard it from God. So they came to Augustown in droves. Union Camp swelled and Bedward's reputation grew until he was the most powerful preacherman in Jamaica. Now, fifteen years later, there was a rumour of a new miracle – and an even greater miracle to come.

Maas Bilby's face trembled and then broke into one of its wide smiles. He stepped fully outside, but said nothing. He took a deep inhale as if to breathe in the dawn, and then he looked up at the colours of the sky.

'Peace and love, Aunt Mathilda,' Maas Bilby suddenly said. It was a belated greeting but full of warmth. 'You right. I believe a good time is coming. Come inside and rest your foot. You must did walk a real long way. Come in!' And he led in the tall, bony woman who seemed unsure as to how to respond to such gallantry.

'Aunt Mathilda?' Norah exclaimed.

'She hear the news!' Bilby offered, almost triumphantly. 'It reach her all de way in Clarendon. Nuh true, Aunt Mathilda? De news travel far already. Tell her. Tell Miss Norah!'

Aunt Mathilda nodded as she sat herself down on a wooden chair. 'Yes. Is true that I hear something. But you all know that news can change with distance. Is better to come and hear things for yourself.' Aunt Mathilda suddenly grimaced. She rubbed her stomach the way old Jamaican women occasionally do. 'Norah, my dear, you have any ginger there?'

Norah rummaged through a basket for a piece of ginger root and handed it to Mathilda with a knife. Mathilda peeled the rough beige skin off of the ginger and then cut the yellow root into small cubes. One by one, she put the cubes into her mouth, chewed and then spat the trash out into the cup of her hands. After a few minutes she seemed settled again.

'As I was saying,' she picked up naturally, 'I is a woman who don't put no trust in carry-go-bring-come news. I come to Augustown to hear things with my own ears, and see things with my own eyes. So please oonoo tell me now what has been happening.'

So Norah told Aunt Mathilda about the floating incident, how Bedward had just flown up to the ceiling with all the sheets still wrapped round him.

Aunt Mathilda whistled. 'You know,' the old woman said, 'once upon a time you used to hear these kinds of things all the while. Yes. All the while. But is plenty years now I don't hear of such a thing – like him is a true Flying African.'

Norah was sceptical. She sucked her teeth. 'You really hear of people floating before?'

Mathilda drew her head back and narrowed her eyes as if hurt by the lack of trust in her niece's voice. 'At my age,' she said haughtily, 'I did know people who did live on bucky estate as slave, and you hear all kinds of things. True true things that you might never believe.'

'Sorry,' Norah whispered. 'I never mean . . .' and the sentence trailed off.

Mathilda nodded. 'The old people used to talk these things. They say many of us was born with the ability to fly, but we lose the gift when we started eating salt. Is like the salt weigh us down. That's why bucky master make sure to feed us salt fish and salt pork and all them things, so that those of us who could fly would lose the gift. But sometimes a man or woman might go into fasting and when-time they lose all the salt from them body, then that time they would start to float. And some of them did float all the way back to the Motherland. Back to Africa. They call them the Flying Africans. Mm-hm. That's what the old people would call them. And it sound to me now like the Shepherd have the same gift.'

They would have continued talking, but there was another sound at the door, louder and more urgent than the gentle stone Aunt Mathilda had used earlier to tap and announce her presence. This time it was the flat of someone's palm banging. Maas Bilby frowned. 'Is what de dickens is going on this morning, eh?'

'Hello!' a voice called from outside.

'Yes, we hear you!' Maas Bilby called back. 'Hold on, man!'

Maas Bilby arced himself out of the chair and walked over to the door. He opened it and the sun was bright in the sky and shining down on the excited face of one of the young boys of Augustown. The boy looked at Maas Bilby, and then, as if ignoring him, stretched his face around him and looked into the house. 'Him coming! Master Bedward coming out of his house now! Oonoo come!' And with that, he ran back out of the yard and up the street.

Maas Bilby turned to Norah and Aunt Mathilda and they all shrugged together, but soon they got up to leave the house. They stepped out into the yard and noticed now the crowd gathering up the road, everyone skipping from foot to foot. Maas Bilby led the way, behind him Aunt Mathilda and behind her Norah, holding firmly onto the hand of Little Irene. As they stepped towards the crowd a neighbour turned to them and gestured them forward. 'He coming soon! Come, man.'

It was as if all of Augustown was outside, lining the thin marl road as if a motorcade was about to pass with King Edward himself at the centre. As the crowd grew larger, the chattering swelled. Then all at once it died. A hush fell.

At the top of the road they could now see a procession of men in dark jackets. There were six deacons from the church, and it was obvious that they were surrounding Bedward. People strained to catch a glimpse of him between the six men, but every now and then he would become clearly visible, rising head and shoulders above the suited gentlemen who encircled him. Then he would fall back. Each time his head appeared, the crowd would gasp, realising that it was the deacons with their hands firmly pressed on his shoulders who were stopping him from rising clean up into the sky. So it was true. The man was flying.

Aunt Mathilda was trembling. She leaned on Maas Bilby for support. It seemed almost comical to Irene, the tall woman leaning on the shorter man. Irene tugged on her mother's skirt. 'Mama! He flying for true.' When Norah turned around, it seemed to the little girl that her mother's eyes were a little wet. Norah lifted her daughter up into her arms so that she could get an even better view of things. 'Yes, baby. You right,' Norah whispered. 'Bedward flying for true.'

Irene watched fascinated as the procession went by. She was impressed by the high, bouncing walk of the preacher-man. She had never seen anything like it, and would never see anything like it again, though she almost did: many years later, after the roof collapsed and the rats had gouged out her eyes, she sat there in the front room of her house while her three nieces and Sister Gilzene gathered around the black and white television set. It was 20 July 1969, and two Yankee fellows were about to step out of a rocket and onto the moon. Ma Taffy listened. The three little girls and the old woman from next door watched as Neil Armstrong took what he said was a small step for man and a giant leap for mankind. It was Sister Gilzene who pressed her face closer to the screen of the television, scrutinising the way these men with the fishbowls over their heads would make a soft step onto the surface of the moon and then bounce right up, the lack of gravity causing them to float. Sister Gilzene held her heart and exclaimed, 'Jesus, son of Mary!'

'What now?' Ma Taffy asked.

'Oh my heavens, Taffy!' Gilzene said. 'If you could only see what I seeing now on this thing here that oonoo call a television. Two man up there in the heavens above us, walking bout, and just so the man-dem make one step, is just so the other step take dem up up up into the air. Is almost like . . .' And she stopped right there, the silence sudden and awkward between them. And though she never completed

70

the sentence, Ma Taffy heard the words as if they had been said, words that opened up a painful old-time story, '. . . is almost like the walk of Bedward. Is like the walk of the flying preacherman.'

8

On that Sunday in December 1920 when William Grant-Stanley showed up at Union Camp for Sunday service, it wasn't that no one knew who he was or what he was about; it wasn't that anyone really credited his cock-and-bull story that his name was Matthias Marcus, and that he was a revivalist come from St Elizabeth all the way to Augustown just to hear the great preacherman preach; it wasn't that anyone believed his feigned surprise that he hadn't heard anything about this business of flying, and that it was just a coincidence that he had showed up on this Sunday of all Sundays.

'Oh my! Flying?' said William Grant-Stanley under his new pseudonym of Matthias Marcus, 'I hadn't heard any such thing. Do tell me!' But *seeya, dear God!* they wanted to exclaim. Who other than uptown people used language such as he was using? And who on the entire island hadn't already heard about Bedward and the floating incident? Even people who lived in Mocho, and the furthest regions of *behind-God-back* had heard. And which revivalist would come to service in a three-piece suit that looked hardly more than a year old, and that you could tell from its cut and fit was made by a professional tailor, more than likely Samuel & Son on King's

Street? It wasn't that revivalist men didn't take great pride in their outfits; but there were suits, and then again, there were suits. And which revivalist would come visiting from far and without even a turban wrapped around his head? And last of all, which man with olive skin and almost straight hair ever had a name like 'Matthias Marcus'? No, sah! Who was he trying to fool? Why did he take them for idiots? They knew straight away that this was just another newspaperman come to spy and report on them. But no one blew his cover. They had become used to this sort of thing.

But if the colour of William Grant-Stanley's skin, and the near straightness of his hair, and the clear Kingston twang of his accent, which sounded nothing like the music of a St Bess patois, and the expensive cut of his suit; if all this did not already make him conspicuous, it hardly helped that he would take out his notebook, glancing to his left and to his right, scribble things in it, and then put it away only to take it out again a moment later. Eventually he just kept the notebook in the middle of his open Bible for easy reach.

Still, no one called him out on his sham. They were too well-mannered for that, yet not so well-mannered as not to have their fun with him, to treat him like the blasted pappy-show into which he had made himself.

Bredda Toby went over and greeted him. 'Bredda Matty?'

'Excuse me?' William Grant-Stanley said, scratching his head.

'Nuh Bredda Matty you say yu name is?'

'No. It's Matthias . . .' he began before understanding. 'Oh yes, yes, of course. I'm Brother . . . Bredda Matty.'

'Well, good to have you here, Bredda Matty. Nice that you come visit we all the way from Saint Bess. Welcome,

73

welcome in de name of Jeezas.' And Bredda Toby slapped him so hard on the back that William Grant-Stanley coughed.

When the service began, Sister Bernadine, who was sitting on Grant-Stanley's right, found every occasion to close her eyes and lean towards him as if being swayed by the Spirit, and whenever she got close to his ears she would shout, 'HALLELUJAH!' which caused the man to jump – his Bible, notebook and pen all clattering to the floor. And then when they began to sing, Deaconess Lorna, who sat on Grant-Stanley's left, pretended she was suddenly possessed by the Spirit and threw herself towards him, and he was forced to catch her. As he held her by the waist, Deaconess Lorna reached back and held his hands on her, and proceeded to rock her pelvis this way and that, inching her way into the aisle, leading the hapless journalist into the middle of the church, trying to dance with his two left feet that were not familiar with the ways of the Spirit, while everyone nodded purposefully to him, 'Holy, Bredda Matty. Holy.'

But then Sister Liz herself went up to the pulpit and said simply, 'Awrite den now. Awrite.' The congregation understood the tone of rebuke in these words, and knew it was time for the malarkey to be done with. They sang the final song of the worship session with a different kind of earnestness which was lost on William Grant-Stanley. Then the prayer was prayed that bridged the first half of the service into the second half, and so finally it was time for the Word, for the sermon from Bedward, who had not yet been seen that morning; who was not sitting in his usual place on the throne-like chair on the stage.

Sister Liz was back in the pulpit. 'My brothers and sisters in de Lord, it good to see so many of you here this Sunday.

Praise be his holy name, Amen. Yes? For the Bible say it is good for us, for bredrens and sistrens to meet together in his Holy Name. Yes? Amen. And this will be a special, special Sunday. I can promise you that. For the Lord has visited upon my family this week in a special, special way. And so now my husband, your Shepherd and Parson, Master Bedward, will come and give the Word and tell you bout this new visitation of the Holy Spirit. But only one thing I have to say to you, my brothers and sisters . . .' and Sister Liz paused and smiled a rare smile, for she was usually quite a stern woman. 'I not a preacher. So the one degge degge thing I have to say is this: we been toiling in the vineyard. We is a people who know wheat and tares. Yes? But de harvest coming. Lift your noses and smell it on the breeze. De harvest coming.' And with that she nodded, stepped off the pulpit and went back to her seat.

The door at the back of the church opened now, and there was a commotion. The six deacons who seemed to walk together like Bedward's bodyguards squeezed themselves through it, all the while trying not to let go of their master. Bedward emerged last, still walking that high, bouncing walk while the deacons firmly held onto him.

All over the church people were whispering, 'Holy! Holy! Holy!' and William Grant-Stanley, trying to get a better view, stood up and craned his neck towards the front of the church. A woman by the name of Miss Lou was sitting behind the journalist with her ward, Gilzene. Miss Lou was now a baptised Christian, but not so very long ago she had been what many would call a loose woman. Though she tried now to be a woman of moderate speech, whenever she was annoyed her loose tongue came back to her and it was she, her view obstructed, who snapped at Grant-Stanley: 'Sit you blasted ass down, whiteman! What you think this is?'

Bedward was now at the pulpit, and the deacons were going through an elaborate operation of wrapping quite heavy chains around his waist. No one had noticed the chains before, lying inert on the stone floor of the church. The chaining complete, the deacons stepped away to the side and Bedward beamed out at the congregation. He held up his hand as if to restore quiet, though no one had said a word. This was as quiet as Union Camp had ever been.

'Now I don't want you to worry too much by what you seeing here, for I know that we is a people who don't take kindly to chains. Yes?' He had the same speech affectation as his wife, this constant seeking out of affirmation at the end of his sentences. Or maybe it was a habit she had picked up from him. 'Chains and we have a terrible, terrible history. But be not dismayed or downhearted, my children, for these chains that you see de brothers wrap round me, they not tying me to no buckra, they only tying me to this earth that God give us to toil on for a time, though he tell us in his Holy Word – amen – that it, too, this earth, shall pass away.

'My brothers and sisters, I come today with a softer heart than de heart that I did come here with last week. You remember last week Sunday I had to speak words of comfort for Sister Mary and Brother Marcus who are here again, bless de both of you . . . you remember they just lose their two sweet children.'

Sister Mary and Brother Marcus nodded.

'And I know all of you did come to church just like me, with a heavy stone resting on yu heart. It is always like that

76

with we. We is a forever cast-down people who need to be lifted up. We is a forever righteous people seeking refuge in de strong tower of de Lord.'

It was too early in the sermon for Amens, so the church members responded by jutting out their lips, nodding their heads and Mm-mming.

'You know, it is not a nice thing at all to have de yutes die before de parents. I know that for myself, for as you all know, me and Sister Liz did lose two of our own lickle ones at a early age.'

'Mm-mmm.'

'Now doctor come to tell we that de two pickney that dead last week – that dem dead from one big, highfalutin' something they calling "dysentery". Yes? But what I am here to tell you this morning – what I never say last week but what we all know deep in we heart – is that those two pickney, those two wonderful lickle angels, dem was murdered!'

A hush fell over the church, and every eye looked up to the pulpit where Bedward had paused dramatically. He reached for a calabash bowl of water and drank a sip. He ran his big pink tongue over his lips and then looked into the expectant faces of the congregation. 'Murdered!' he repeated and shook his head. 'Murdered by this country! Murdered by de government. Murdered by de governor man himself.'

'Mm-mmm!'

'Listen to what I telling you, my children! No pickney who born with high colour in this country, or who born to sit in high chair, who born to high-society people – none of dem not deading from no dysentery . . .'

'Oh, no!'

'Dem not deading from no mosquito bite . . .'

'No, sah!'

'. . . or from rat bite or from drinking dutty water, or from whatever else dem tell we dat that fi wi pickney always be deading from. Fi we pickney dead because dem born low – dem born so low to de ground that de grave just reach cross fi dem and pull dem in just so.'

Bedward clapped a hand to his lips and shook his head as if he had surprised himself. It was a gesture the church was used to, but it was still effective. The church too was silent, each man and woman shaking his or her own head and contemplating their collective lowness. Bedward let this feeling swell in the church and then said in a small voice – a whisper, really – 'But blessed is we who born low and live low, for we shall be lifted up!'

Now it was time for an *Amen!*

'I said, WE SHALL BE LIFTED UP!'

More people now: 'Amen!'

'That is why I come this morning with my heart so soft, soft as a feather I telling you, so soft because I know in my spirit that de time of lifting is nigh! WE SHALL BE LIFTED UP UP UP UP UP! Like de blessed saviour who dem put on de cross, tinking dem was putting him down, but dem end up lifting him up, up, up, all de way to de Father's arms! I need somebody to say Amen!'

Everyone now was shouting *Amen!* and *Hallelujah!* and some people were standing on their feet, waving the pieces of cloth they had brought with them for such moments.

Bedward wiped his shiny face with a rag. 'I glad to see de church pack this morning, and I know so many of you is out here because news of a miraculous thing has come to you. Yes? Well, let me tell you now, from my own mouth, de stories you been hearing . . . dem is true.'

'Amen!'

'God is doing a new thing, my children! A miraculous-take-we-out-of-Egypt-and-part-de-Red-Sea thing! A redemptive-dip-we-in-de-water-and-pull-we-out-clean thing! Gawwwwd is doing an uplifting thing. A lift-we-out-of-dungle-and-high-into-de-clouds thing! We don't have to wait and wait and wait and sing Sankey till we dead. Dat time is now on de horizon. I telling you dis morning, it is nigh!'

'Yes, Lord!'

'December thirty-first, my children. December thirty-first. Dat is de day. Tell de people dem all bout. Shout it from de mountain top. December thirty-first. Come ye all to Augus-town, and there shall you see a demonstration of de mighty powers of Jehovah Gawwwd. December thirty-first. If you born low and black and poor, den dat is de day of glory. But if you born high and white and with a gold spoon into yu mouth, well, den dat is de day of terror and judgement and weeping and wailing and gnashing of teeth. Oh, glory to God!'

'Yes!'

'I going to rise up to heaven, my children. Yes. Yes! Dis same black, low-born and low-rated man you see stand up in front of you with de heap of chain wrap round him belly, him same one, me, Alexander Bedward, Shepherd of Augustown, I going to rise up into de skies like Elijah and moresomever, I staying dere for three days! Three days will I walk bout in heaven and shake hands with Moses and Abra-ham and sit down with Jesus. And when-time I come back, I coming with lightning in my hands and dis wicked town name Kingston shall see a ruination worse dan earthquake or fire. Oh, blessed be de name of our God!'

William Grant-Stanley was writing furiously in his note-book, but no one paid him any mind. Bedward continued, 'My children . . . if you have righteousness into yu heart, now is not a time to fear. Now is a time to be joyful. Now is a time to walk with your head hold up high. Dis thing that is nigh, dis thing that is close at hand is a blessed thing. A wonderful thing. For you remember that Bredda Sam Sharp did try to rise up out of Babylon, but it never did work out fi him. And when I was just a lickle boy of six years old, Deacon Bogle try again to rise, but dem take him to yonder gallows and heng him. But dis time, dis time it going to happen. Dis time, all de black and white rascals of dis coun-try, should be fraid. Dis time, all de big money people of dis country should be fraid! Dis time, Governor Leslie Probyn who sit down as comfortable as Miss Thomas puss up dere in King's House, him should be fraid, fraid, fraid! But you, O righteous and downtrodden people – you have nothing to fraid for. A low-born blackman is going to rise up over Babylon. So tell me now . . . oonoo ready?'

9

Calm, rational, even-tempered, cool as a Scottish summer. That's how Leslie Probyn liked to think of himself. These were the qualities he had worked to cultivate as a colonial administrator. But today those words seemed far away. He was infuriated. Despite the mahogany-bladed fan whirring above his head, and the louvred windows of his large office flung open to let in a cool breeze, he was sweating profusely. He was unused to sweat. Though white and pot-bellied and having lived the past many years in countries whose climates were so unlike his native England – Sierra Leone, Nigeria, Grenada, Barbados and now Jamaica – he had always been able to keep his perspiration in check by the sheer force of his will. He asserted a cool stronger than the humidity that pressed around him. When inspecting the guards, for instance, decked out in his colonial uniform, his thick jacket and trousers, the various medals and insignia of office weighing down his shirt, and on his head a helmet with white plumes of feathers bursting out from its top, he would take pleasure in stopping before the most nervous guard, observing as beads of sweat sprouted on the poor guard's forehead then rolled down, and all the while Probyn himself would remain as powder-dry as a withered corpse. *You think this place make only for blackman? Eh?* He thought the words in his head, but would never say them aloud. He took a perverse pleasure in mentally practising the pidgin language of whatever place he was posted to. *Look at me and look at you, nah! Like yu out to drown in yu owna sweat!* And Probyn imagined that, after a time, a measure of respect and awe would emanate from the guard towards him, a kind of concession of his right to be there and to govern. Thus satisfied, he would nod and continue his inspection.

But today was different. Tributaries of perspiration ran down from the governor's forehead onto his clothes, while sweat stains were spreading out from his armpits at an alarming rate, threatening to consume his entire shirt. He had already begun to unbutton the shirt, and would soon call Mr Peabody to fetch him a replacement.

'Damn Yankee! What gives him the right?' he muttered as he turned another page of the book that was causing this great profusion, opening up his usually closed pores and causing his body to drain onto itself.

Jamaica was the hardest assignment he had been given so far. Three hurricanes in three years – bam-bam-bam – had not so much paved the road for his arrival as gouged out that road and filled it with potholes. A flattened St Mary meant that the island, banana country that it was supposed to be, had not actually seen a ripe variety of the fruit since 1915. Sugar cane had fared no better. Waterlogged fields meant that whatever crop came to harvest was all too fresh and virtually useless. And this was not the half of it. The economic tensions paled in comparison to the social tension. The island was on edge. You could feel it. Probyn had arrived to find the fairer-skinned Jamaicans desperate for a governor who would bring back slavery – in all but name, of course – insisting that the blacks were now so completely out of control that they posed a great danger not just to white Jamaicans but even to themselves. On the other hand, the darker-skinned Jamaicans felt that not much had changed since slavery. They wanted a govern-or who could give them freedom in more than just name: better wages, for starters, and the right to vote, and laws that would protect them from abusive employers. In a sense, it was all par for the course. If not with the same intensity, Probyn had experienced tensions of a similar na-ture in every post he had worked in so far. But if he ex-uded calm, it was because he internalised everything. He suppressed things, making him an altogether dangerous man. His calm demeanour was like that of a volcano – a seeming tranquillity on the surface, but something hot and bubbling underneath. If it was easy for him to absorb the general tensions in a society, it was harder for him to deal with criticism directed at him and his administration, which is why the book he was reading was causing such an eruption.

He had been given it the night before at a party in Irish Town. It was one of those houses that opened onto a huge verandah, and the verandah then opened onto a wide green lawn. Nowhere he could think of did verandahs quite like the colonies, and none of the colonies did verandahs quite like Jamaica. He knew it was the thing he would miss most when it was time for him to be reassigned. The garden had been full of birds of paradise, bougainvillea and the red poinsettia that signalled the Christmas season. It was a pleas-ant evening, and with the help of the sherry he was sipping,

Probyn was inclined to think of these flowers as more beautiful than any English rose.

He had been ensconced in conversation with the hostess of the night. As protocol dictated, Mr Peabody, his secretary and assistant, stood to one side. Probyn was complimenting the hostess on the evening and she, with appropriate deference, was thanking His Excellency for gracing them with his presence. Out of the corner of his eye, Probyn spotted Richard Azaar stomping in. He was a brash businessman whom Probyn didn't particularly like, but he was powerful, and so the governor knew he had to tolerate him. Azaar was clutching a book in one hand and his wife in the other; he held both of them like trophies.

'Leslie! Leslie, my good man!' Azaar shouted from across the room. Probyn grimaced at the familiarity. Azaar stomped his way towards the group. He was now holding the book above his head. 'Leslie! Have you read this? I brought this copy just for you! Didn't I, Diana? Didn't I say we would surely see Leslie tonight, and I had to put this book in his hands?'

His wife nodded. 'Yes, you did say that, darling.'

Crass bastard! Probyn thought to himself.

'Have you read it yet, Leslie? Imagine, this is how these damn Yanks see us. Have you read it?'

'Mr Azaar, might you be so kind as to actually show me the piece of literature you're referring to? I may have read it; I may not have. I'm rather in the dark here.'

But Probyn already had a fair idea of what the book was. Between 1917 and 1918, a fellow by the name of Harry A. Franck had been skipping from Caribbean island to Caribbean island. Now, two years later, he had published a book

84

about those travels, *Roaming Through the West Indies*. It had been creating quite a stir.

Azaar shoved the book into the governor's hands. 'This book, man! For godsake. This book. "*Roaming Through the Blasted West Indies*". You have to read it, and then we have to talk. And let me tell you what the awful thing is. The fucker is bloody right. Excuse my language, ladies. But every goddamn word of it! I'm tired of saying it, you know, Leslie. And mark you, you're not the first governor I've said it to but these Jamaican negroes are spoiling things for everybody!'

Probyn flinched. To his eyes, Azaar was a mulatto man. In England he would most certainly be considered 'coloured'. His father was Syrian; his mother looked the same, but was actually some mixture of white and black. But Probyn knew that despite this mixed heritage, and Azaar's olive skin and dark eyes, he lived on an island in which he was considered lily white. Indeed, Azaar would be offended if you suggested he was anything but. His wealth only confirmed his island whiteness, as did his position as President of the Chamber of Commerce, and always in Azaar's mind it was the blacks who were ruining things for him.

'Gentlemen! Gentlemen!' cried the hostess, trying to intervene. 'This is not a night for politics.' But these were words she often said and, as always, she was being disingenuous. Mrs Selena Jackman quite liked the idea that her house was a place where important things happened and important conversations were had.

'Yes, I know, Selena! I know. But just hear me out for a second. We have to think of this island like a brand. Like Wray and Nephew – you know what I mean. Brand Jamaica, that's what I say. And these negroes, they spoiling the brand.

85

Their behaviour these days is just getting more and more obproperous!'

'Obstreperous,' his wife corrected him meekly.

'Yes, yes . . . whatever the goddamn word is! You know what I mean. Read the thing, Leslie, and you'll see that it's an embarrassment to all of us. A real embarrassment.'

'I think you will find, Mr Azaar, that the negroes will be disinclined to change their behaviour if there is no real benefit to them doing so. Certainly that was my experience in West Africa . . .'

'Yes, exactly, Leslie! Exactly! Like bloody Africans. These Jamaican negroes have to change their behaviour if they want to progress.'

'That wasn't quite my point . . .'

'Well, we have to talk through these things. And soon, Leslie. Soon. As a matter of fact, how is tomorrow?'

'I'm afraid my schedule might not permit—'

But already Mr Azaar had turned to Mr Peabody. 'Mr Peabody, how is the governor's schedule looking for tomorrow?'

Mr Peabody, who had been working at King's House for the best part of a decade, and who had watched three governors come and go, was immediately deferential to Mr Azaar. 'His Excellency can accommodate you at eleven a.m., Mr Azaar.'

'Fantastic, Mr Peabody! Fantastic! Put me in for that time.' He turned back to the governor and clapped him on the shoulder. 'So I'll see you tomorrow, Leslie. And read the damn thing. Outrageous man. Outrageous!'

Sir Leslie Probyn had therefore already been bristling with anger from the night before, and this morning – sitting in his King's House office, reading the chapter that this uppity

86

mulatto had instructed him, the governor, to read – was giving him palpitations.

The insolence of nearly all the British West Indies reaches its zenith in Kingston . . . The town is dismal, disagreeable and unsafe for self-respecting white women at any hour; by night it is virtually abandoned to the lawless black hordes that infest it. Weak gas-lights give it scarcely a suggestion of illumination; swarms of negroes shuffle through the hot dust, cackling their silly laughter, shouting their obscenity, heckling, if not attacking, the rare white men who venture abroad, love-making in perfect indifference to the proximity of other human beings, while the pompous black policemen look on without the slightest attempt to quell the disorder.

The white residents of Kingston seem to live in fear of the black multitude that make up the great bulk of the population. When hoodlums and rowdies jostle them on the street, they shift aside with a slinking air; even when black hooligans cling to the outside of street-cars pouring out obscene language, the white men do not shield their wives and daughters beside them by so much as raising their voice in protest . . .

The few white officials are slow, antiquated, precedence-ridden, in striking contrast to the young and bustling, if sometimes poorly informed rulers of our own dependencies. Indeed, a journey to the West Indies is apt to cause the American to rearrange his notions of the relative efficiency of the English, and the French or ourselves, as colonizers. We are sadly in need of a Colonial Office and a corps of trained officials to administer what we dislike to call our colonies, but even our deserving Democrats, or Republicans, as the case may be, scarcely hamper the development of our dependencies as thoroughly as do its medieval-minded rulers that of Jamaica[1].

---

1 Harry Franck, *Roaming Through the West Indies*

Probyn took the book and hurled it across the room. It found the large black and white photograph of King Edward and shattered the frame. There was a banging at the door.

'Your Excellency? Is everything OK?'

'It's all right, Mr Peabody. Just give me a moment. And fetch me a shirt, please.'

'Yes, sir,' Mr Peabody said from behind the door.

Probyn sighed. He still hadn't forgiven the man for his betrayal the night before. Remembering the 11 a.m. meeting, he looked up at the clock. Twenty minutes. Probyn crossed the room with a sheet of paper. He knelt and tried to sweep the splinters onto the sheet. He winced as one of the shards pierced his index finger. A bright bubble of blood appeared on the tip. He licked it away and pressed the finger against his trousers to stop the bleeding.

There was a knock on the door again. 'Your Excellency?'

'Yes, Mr Peabody, come in.'

Mr Peabody entered, observed the shattered frame but said nothing. 'Your shirt, sir,' handing a fresh white shirt to the governor, 'and your eleven o'clock is early. Shall I send them in?'

Them?! Probyn tried to keep his annoyance in check. 'No. I will not be ready to see them until eleven.' He pointed to the splinters. 'Please get someone to clear that up.'

'Yes, sir.'

Peabody disappeared, and Probyn peeled the soaked shirt off his body. He stood directly under the fan for a moment and then put the fresh shirt on. A maid arrived and cleared away the debris, and at ten past eleven Azaar and two other gentlemen were ushered into the governor's office. Probyn knew that the Richard Azaar he was about to speak with was a slightly different man from the one he had met the night before. There was nothing jovial about this Azaar. This was the hard-as-nails businessman.

'Leslie,' Azaar greeted him. 'I believe you already know Tommy Delgado and Keith Thompson from the Chamber as well.' The men nodded, shook hands and took a seat. Probyn knew the two extra men would say little during the meeting. They were there as a kind of decoration, and a show of power. He, Richard Azaar, could invite whomever he wanted to the governor's office.

'So how can I help you, Richie?' Probyn began, almost spitefully. He had never called Richard Azaar by his first name, let alone the diminutive 'Richie', but he enjoyed watching the man squirm and he knew it was a good tactic to start such meetings by throwing people off balance.

Richard Azaar adjusted his tie. 'Your Excellency,' he began more appropriately, 'we could talk till the bloody cows come home about all the awful things happening in this country – the hooliganism and rampant disorder and all the things I'm sure you read about in that fellow's book. Disgraceful. But we're busy men, so let me get to the most pressing matter at hand. We're concerned about this fellow, Bedward. The one from Augustown. You've heard of him, of course.'

Aah, Probyn thought. He should have guessed. If it wasn't this Marcus Garvey fellow, it was Alexander Bedward. Both men seemed to have a knack for getting under the skins of high Jamaican society. 'Yes, I've heard of Mr Bedward.'

'And you been hearing this malarkey about him going to fly! You ever heard such stupidness?'

Mr Delgado and Mr Thompson tittered. Probyn kept a straight face.

'Mr Azaar. We've all heard about Bedward's lunatic prophecy. But I'm not sure why this is the most pressing matter.'

Azaar slammed his hand on the table, causing even the governor to jump. 'What you mean, you don't see why this is a pressing matter?' he bellowed. 'Look here, Mr Governor. With all due respect, you don't seem to understand how things work on this island. This is the Christmas season, you see, and just last Saturday I had to close my store early – and Tommy and Keith here will tell you the same thing.' Mr Delgado and Mr Thompson nodded their support. 'We had to close down early because not enough bloody workers showing up. Left, right and centre they were all quitting. And you know for what?'

'Pray tell.'

'So they can go to bloody Augustown! I've never seen anything like it. The set of fools lining up behind this fucking madman, all of them marching to that dirty little village as if it was some kind of Mecca. If you ask me, they have some strong kind of African obeah working down there, drawing all these innocent people to it.'

'Mr Azaar,' Probyn began with a smile, 'I appreciate your passion.' This was British insincerity, of course. He was mocking the man for a passion he read as foolish and immature. The governor's voice was, as usual, calm, but it now held within it a measure of steel. He did not appreciate this mulatto man banging on his table as if to intimidate him, and therefore felt the need to reassert his authority. 'Still, I'm not sure what can be done here. Surely you're not worried that Mr Bedward is truly going to fly to heaven and come back with lightning to smite us? And as far as the law is concerned, there's nothing against him proclaiming his intention to fly – however ridiculous we know those claims to be. We're rational human beings, Mr Azaar. Time and gravity. Those will be the downfall of Bedward. Time and gravity.'

'Businesses being forced to close during the Christmas season! Surely this is a national crisis?' This was Mr Delgado, whose face had gone very red.

'Your Excellency,' said Mr Azaar. 'I'm not worried that Bedward is going to fly. Of course I'm not. But what he has set off is very dangerous – dangerous to this country's economy and dangerous to our morality. And all under your watch. You mark my words, Mr Governor, something else is brewing under it all. Some kind of uprising, some kind of rebellion. Just walk outside and you can feel it in the air.'

'Gentlemen, I have the advantage of having lived in many colonies. So believe me when I tell you this: that feeling is always in the air.'

Azaar lifted his fist as if to bang it on the table again, but caught the warning flash in Probyn's eyes. He relaxed his hand and adjusted his tie again.

'So you're saying that's it, then? All these black hooligans and no-gooders gathering together in Augustown and plotting God-he-knows-what, leading astray the few good Christian workers we have in our stores, and the only response from King's House is to shrug – to turn your hands up in the air and say, so it guh? That's what you're saying?'

Governor Probyn looked directly at Mr Azaar but made no reply. His face had become its cool, sweatless mask again. While the three men in front of him grew red and anxious and bothered, Probyn stared them down, unflappable.

Mr Azaar tried again. 'Mr Governor, sir. Let me talk plain.

You don't like me. You see me as a brash little uncouth man. I know that. Of course I know that. And to be honest, I couldn't give a flying fuck what you Limeys think of us. After you leave this bloody island, I'll still be here. But what I'm telling you is much bigger than whether you like me or not. Something dangerous is brewing on this island, and it has to be stopped. And if you want to stop it, sir, then you have to stop Bedward. Mark my words. If you don't stop it, then worse things are going to be written about your governorship than what that American fellow wrote in that book. Trust me.' And Richard Azaar shrugged magnificently as if depositing the weight of the world in the governor's lap. 'Sir, I've taken enough of your time. Good morning, Mr Governor.' Richard Azaar nodded his head and left the office. Mr Delgado and Mr Thompson hastily shook the hand of the governor and ran to catch up with him.

10

In Augustown back then, there were many kinds of stories: Bible stories and Anancy stories; book stories and susu stories; stories read by lamplight and stories told by moonlight. But always there was this divide between the stories that were written and stories that were spoken – stories that smelt of snow and faraway places, and stories that had the smell of their own breath.

It had been believed – in an unsaid sort of a way – that a story would never be written about Augustown, but this all changed with the advent of the flying preacherman. The people added to their taxonomy of stories a new kind: the newspaper story. And this seemed to fall somewhere in between what was written and what was spoken, for as they waited for 31 December to come, they would gather each night in the churchyard and someone would roll out the *Jamaica Gleaner* and, like an Anancy storyteller, would read to them the story of themselves. It hardly mattered that these stories were mostly negative – that they were being mocked. It mattered only that they had been noticed and written about.

Bedward himself would be among his flock as these newspaper stories were read out each night. He was comfortable now, floating back and forth above the crowd like a ministering angel. And perhaps it was this nightly demonstration of his flying power that made the reading of these stories such a jovial affair, because Augustown knew something that these newspaper people did not know; they could see what the rest of Jamaica refused to see.

The stories they read on such nights included this one:

The Gleaner
Kingston, Jamaica
Wednesday, December 15, 1920

What Phase Is This?

He began as Bedward, metamorphosed into Father Bedward, and now has attained the dignity of 'Lord' Bedward. He commenced as one who could stare at the sun as it rode in the Heavens in all its majesty and glory at noontide. He now aspires to ascend to Heaven like Elijah, possibly in a chariot of fire, but at all events amidst the shouts and acclamations of his followers who at this moment profess to be preparing for the Judgment Day. Thus has Mr Bedward evolved from a simple country peasant into a religious leader and prophet of thousands, and now one is wondering whether we have reached the last phase of Bedwardism, or whether we should expect any further development in the mentality and position of this interesting person.

As our special representative, W.G.S., has graphically described in our impressions of yesterday and today, Bedward has been uttering strange and weird predictions for some little time, and these have obtained an almost island-wide circulation. Just as nearly thirty years ago Bedward was alleged to have asserted that a Black Wall was about to overwhelm the White Wall of Jamaica – which words might have

94

meant anything, but probably meant nothing — so now he is alleged to be prophesying woe and lamentation, the destruction of the city of Kingston, the end of the world, universal ruin, and the translation of himself to Heaven. This last would be a most interesting occurrence. We have never seen anyone translated to Heaven, but of course the 'Lord' Bedward is able to fall back on precedent. Enoch, a biblical character, is supposed to have been caught up in the skies without suffering disease. Elijah was also transported to the higher regions by chariots and horses of fire. We believe that at various times since then, other prophets and men of religious note have given out that they were too great to perish like ordinary mortals, but merely disappear from Earth. Empedocles, the Greek philosopher, is believed to have thrown himself into Etna, in the hope of deluding his followers that he had passed from earth in a manner mysterious and supernatural. It may be that Mr Bedward has read about Empedocles. He certainly is acquainted with the history of Enoch and Elijah. So he fixes the 31st for his translation, for Kingston's destruction, and for various other happenings, and many of his followers who are always looking for the end of the world or some other extraordinary occurrence, have now made Augustown, a scene of wilder fanaticism than before, a scene of religious revelry which degenerates into orgies and reduces those who take part in them into corybants almost below the level of rational human beings.

The 31st is not far distant, and the fools that have sold their properties in anticipation of the translation of Lord Bedward and the consummation of the world will assuredly be regretting their precipitate action before many weeks have passed. If their awakening to a sense of their folly would mean the end of Bedwardism, we should not at all regret the sacrifice that they have made. But will anything mean the end of Bedwardism for many years to come? When the day passes and Bedward finds that the chariots and horses of fire, or

95

perhaps the super-six automobile of flame, has not arrived on time, what will he do? There is always suicide as a resort: one can always die. But the most of us have no desire to die, and Lord Bedward is not at all likely to adopt a common and ordinary means of leaving a world which has witnessed his great efforts towards its reformation. When therefore, he finds that no conveyance has been sent for him from Heaven, he will probably have a new revelation. He may then explain to his followers that the world has been given another chance, and that he has been commanded to remain in it for a little longer in order to bring more souls to be washed in the water of Augustown. He will be implicitly believed for the people who flock to him desire to believe in his mission, are intent upon subscribing to any doctrine he may enunciate so long as it appeals to their febrile religious emotions and erotic impulses. If Bedward died tomorrow another prophet would arise in his place. His baptisms would still be carried on. Crowds would still make the pilgrimage to Augustown and every now and then a new prophesy would be proclaimed. For Bedward and his like deal in the primitive stuff of religious emotionalism. Fervid gesticulation, frenzied dances, wild shouts and cries, vague utterances of presumable terrible import − all these appeal to undisciplined, uninstructed people. So Bedwardism will continue even if Bedward disappears. It will continue until the people are sufficiently educated to perceive the folly of the claims of a so-called prophet, and have developed a sufficient sense of social pride to feel ashamed at being connected with an orgiastic revival of primitive superstitions.

And also this:

The Gleaner
Kingston, Jamaica
December 30, 1920

96

Bedwardites Look For the 'Ascension' To-Morrow

The followers of the prophet Bedward, the self-styled 'Lord and Master' of Augustown, are confidently expecting his ascension on Friday of this week, and the destruction of Kingston as a climax to the event. Meanwhile the poor misguided people are flocking to the village in large numbers with their offerings, but of what possible use these will be to their 'Lord', who is to depart to regions unknown, it is hard for even them to say.

A visitor at Augustown yesterday morning had a novel experience. He arrived at the camp at about 9'30 o'clock, and approaching the bungalow, in the verandah of which was Mr Bedward with numerous followers crowded about, he was accosted by a man with the query, 'Do you want to see him?' Accepting the invitation which was just what the stranger wanted, he went in following a path which was made for him through the throng. Arrived at the top of the few steps, and in front of the 'prophet', a woman mad with fanatical zeal rushed at him and held him by the collar.

His interviewer, realizing that a personal struggle might have ended in others joining the affair, perhaps with disastrous consequences, retained his presence of mind and requested the 'prophet' to ask 'his disciples to be more gentle!' He approached 'Lord' Bedward, who, sitting in front of his house with his stick in his hand, dressed in a white tunic kind of coat, white trousers and shirt, his feet unshod, with his grizzly hair and beard turning white, surrounded by a large crowd, alternately gesticulating, murmuring and quiet, presented a striking appearance.

'Good morning, Mr Bedward' was the stranger's first essay. But the 'Lord' treated this salutation with contempt. The visitor perceived what was lacking and hurriedly amended his greeting, saying with

97

effusion while he offered his hand, 'Hail, Lord and Masterful Bedward! The morning greets you!' This warmed the prophet up a bit and his face was illumined with a smile. He was evidently pleased with the suffix to 'Master', and he arose and proceeded to give a long, rambling, disjointed account of his history. It was difficult to understand him, but amidst very undignified language his interviewer gathered that 'Lord' Bedward had a grievance against the Governor and other gentlemen, that he was the 'Son of God' and therefore claimed the title 'Lord and Master'. Then came the grand climax of his ascension, which he still maintains will come off at 10 o'clock on Friday morning, immediately followed by the destruction of the city when 'white and black rascals shall perish'.

This harangue had the effect of working up his followers to a high state of frenzy, and the stranger thinking that discretion was the better part of valour, his sole aim now was to make a speedy departure. Therefore he did not question the 'prophet' as to the manner of his flight through the air. He bade the 'Lord and Master' a polite goodbye, and shook hands with him again.

The second handshake was heartier, but the 'stranger within the gates' was not yet to be released for the prophet had much more to say, most of which seemed quite incoherent. The references to the destruction of white and black rascals (particularly the former) continued with the rise and fall of the 'prophet's' oratory, which was punctuated by the murmurings of his people, a quotation from the Bible now and again being taken up by his most well-read disciples. However, the opportunity came at last and the stranger asked if he might be present at the ascension, at the same time holding out his hand which was now clasped quite heartily. The stranger's parting words were, 'Be good to your flock.'

Passing, apparently unconcernedly through the crowd, the stranger stopped opposite the large building he took to be Bedward's church.

Accosting a disciple as to whether it was Mr Bedward's church he soon realised his lapsus linguae, for followers crowded round shouting, 'Jesus Christ!' 'Lord and Master!' 'the Son of God!' Our friend saw it was time to make himself scarce, so without further enquiries about the 'prophet's' church, he quickened his pace and left the excited people to themselves and their 'lord'.

On his way from Augustown, questions put to 'Pilgrims to the new Mecca' elicited the fact of their great faith in Bedward. The possibility of their 'ascending Lord' revising his plans, would be regarded by many as the will of God. The last episode of the stranger was the reply of a girl some way from Augustown, from whom information had been requested as to the way to take back to the Hope Road. The conversation revealed her belief in the prophet's genuineness. Shown a New Testament with the statement that she could read in it all about Anti-Christ, the girl only shrugged her shoulders and muttered something unintelligible.

The stranger's convictions are that many of the prophet's followers are probably more fanatic than he is himself. Their enthusiasm might result in anything at the word of the 'Master'. The whole affair shows lack of education in the poor people who follow blindly much as though they lived four or five hundred years ago in the 'witch doctor' superstition of African wilds. After the disillusionment, some may remain resigned to their fate, and many will be disappointed, some bitterly, and this in many cases, after having disposed of their earthly possessions with no regard for the future.

Finally, although Bedward was not more abusive than usual, his lurid language becoming lost to the interviewer in its general incoherence, steps should be taken at least by the authorities to put a stop to the obscenities which many witnesses can testify accompany the prophet's ministrations.

11

One morning back then, in 1920, a little before the whole
flying thing had started, a young and barely pubescent Gilzene was getting ready to step out of the house, wearing her
schoolgirl's uniform of a khaki skirt and white blouse. Her
guardian, Miss Lou, looked the child up and down, her gaze
lingering especially on the now orange-sized mounds jutting
out from what had only recently been the flat plank of the
child's chest. She frowned. The child's body was maturing.

'Look here, pickney,' Miss Lou said, her arms now akimbo, 'I see there that yu getting to a certain age.' Her gaze
was still firmly fixed on the child's breasts, and she made this
– her gaze – do the explaining of what the particular age in
question was. 'But make I tell yu something,' Miss Lou continued. 'If yooouuu ever so force-ripe to come home with
belly . . . hmph . . . mi a guh cut it right outa yu myself!
And yu coulda bleed to deat' fi all I care!'

Gilzene turned a confused face towards Miss Lou. The
young girl's rectangular eyes tried but failed to grow past
their natural geometry into wide circles. 'Ma'am?' she asked.
And it was only then, at this simple question, that Miss Lou
took a good look at her ward – not just at her growing
breasts, but at everything else. And it dawned on her in

quite a profound way that this speech she had just given was unnecessary. The child who stood before her was ugly. Spectacularly so. How had she not noticed this before? If anything was going to protect this girl's virginity, her looks would. Miss Lou was suddenly moved with an incredible pity for the child, who she would henceforth refer to in conversations as 'de poor wretched soul'. She reached out and held Gilzene's hand. 'Nuh mind me, darling. Gwaan school and study yu book like a good girl. Yes, man. Gwaan.' And she ushered Gilzene out into the street.

Miss Lou watched the figure of the little girl disappear down the road. She tutted to herself once more. 'Mmmmmm. Dat one nuh pretty at all, at all, at all. She descend from me, yes, but dem looks weh she got is not mines. Not from my fambily.'

Miss Lou was not Gilzene's mother, nor was she the child's grandmother – the more typical family arrangement, grandparents raising their grandchildren. In fact, Miss Lou was Gilzene's great-grandmother. What was especially unusual was the youthful age of Miss Lou. At the time of Gilzene's birth, she was still a few months shy of her fiftieth. To be a great-grandmother at the age of forty-nine required, for many, a fair bit of head-scratching, but all the addition and subtraction led each budding mathematician of Augustown to the inevitable conclusion: that Gilzene was the latest in a line of women from whom nothing good could come; women who were drawn from an early age, and in a selfdestructive way, to men; women of whom it was widely whispered, *Dem so much as look pon cocky, even when it lie dung dead in man trousers, and bam!! Dem get belly just so!*

When Miss Lou entered her sixties, she went willingly to

101

an event no one could have convinced her to go to before – an open-air crusade – and she made an appropriate spectacle of herself, cowbawling her way down the aisle to the repentance corner. Her baptism one week later in the waters of the Mona River sealed the deal. She had found religion. Now she was determined to transform herself into a proper and dignified old lady, as befitted her age. She began to sit in the sun every day, willing her still black hair to start greying. She also began to affect the stooped walk of someone stricken with arthritis. She was determined to raise her now pubescent great-granddaughter in a different way than the other women of her family had been raised, and so the hypocritical harangue with which she had lambasted Gilzene that morning had been rehearsed for weeks before it was finally delivered.

But long before Miss Lou had recognised her great-granddaughter's ugliness, Gilzene had been aware of it herself. It had been pointed out to her by her fellow students, by teachers and even by complete strangers on the road. And this pointing out had never been done in a cruel or malicious way, but rather as a simple matter of observation, or as an easy way to differentiate her from others. 'Ugly gyal!' vendors might call to her, or school acquaintances who either didn't know or had forgotten her name. So Gilzene understood her ugliness in much the way that she understood that Tuesday followed Monday, or that one plus one was equal to two. That is to say, she knew it as a simple and a shruggable fact. She did not feel down about her ugliness, or indeed, that ugliness was aesthetically inferior to beauty.

But if Gilzene lacked anything in looks, she made up for it with talent. Each evening, Miss Lou would present her knees to Gilzene – the knees which she had convinced herself had suddenly been stricken with arthritis – and she would ask the young girl to rub them down with bay rum. As the girl performed this nightly duty, the Augustown evening now smelling of menthol and pimento, Miss Lou would inevitably instruct the girl further, 'Sing something fi mi, nuh!' And Gilzene, who would have anticipated this instruction all day, would sing whatever little song she had been secretly practising – a jamma, a shey-shey, a Sunday School chorus, a folk song they both knew or even a little tune she had made up herself.

Her voice was not typical. Hers was not the rich alto one might expect from a churchified young woman in Augustown – not that gruffly textured sound that had in it the feel of planting cane or walking long distances, and that had at its centre a kind of brokenness which was where all its power sprang from. No. That was not Gilzene. There was something rather birdlike about her voice. It was a clean and sweet soprano that would seem delicate at first, but which could rise to a power which would always take you by surprise. Though she made no conscious attempt to hide her gift, it remained something of a secret for quite some time, known only to Miss Lou and the neighbours – Maas Bilby, Miss Norah and their little girl Irene, who, whenever they heard Gilzene sing, would open the windows wide as if to let the night air in.

Little wonder, then, that on 31 December 1920 it was Sister Gilzene who began to sing the preacherman up, up, up towards the clouds.

Back on her verandah, sixty-two years into the future, Ma

103

Taffy is stretching her mind to remember it all. She tells Kaia the final portion of the story like this:

'So the Christmas we never care about come and go, and then the day we was really waiting on come at last. And I swear is like a breeze did come down that morning and sweep through Augustown and replace the smell of shit with something sweeter, like morning dew. I was just a little girl – a little beenie thing, but I was among people who did find again that thing that made them people. And them ones that my Aunt Mathilda did tell us bout – the old ones who used to be slave people – well, they was there too, come now to see a true true Flying African, and they say how glad they was that they manage to live to see a day like this.

'When Master Bedward come out, I feel something big trying to rise out of my little body, and I think everybody was feeling it too – like we never had so much love for anything before. Him was just so big and black and beautiful in them shining white robes, white as if them did wash in the cleanest river. The deacons lead him over to the big saman tree that I believe is still there, and then they let him go. Bedward allow himself of float up to the tallest branch, and then he hold on and smile down like he was proud of all of we.

'They form a circle round the tree, making space so the old people and the little ones like me could come up in front and see. No one was saying anything or making a sound. There was just that thing happening in each of our hearts, like it was breaking and healing and breaking and healing. And then, still without making a sound, a sister wheel into the middle of the circle, and she turn and she dip and then she look up at Bedward and she bow deep, and then wheel back out, and then all the women was doing it – my mother, Norah, and Aunt Mathilda – all of them wheeling and bowing, but quiet, quiet, without grunting or trumping or speaking in tongues, and Bedward, he was just nodding and smiling at everybody. This go on for a while. Nobody did feel impatient. It feel like this was something we had waited on for so long, it was OK just to sit down and consider it.

'I hear them before I did even see them. Babylon boys. Maybe a hundred of them, with their black boots and their batons and their long rifles, marching up to Union Camp like they coming to fight war. And all it was, was the sound of them boots on the stones, but it was so loud, and that is when the day start to spoil. The governor himself was there too – a red, piggish face man in front of them all, walking there in the sunhot but not bussing a sweat, and when I look on him I feel I was looking at a corpse.

'The old people especially was nervous. One woman start to cry, "This always happen! Always, always happen! That's why I tell you I never want to come! Cause this always happen!"

'Some people try to hush her up but she wouldn't stop, and suddenly we was breaking up, like we wasn't people together no more. I know I was just a girl, but I tell you, Kaia, I could feel us moving away from each other. And even Master Bedward up there in the saman tree, there was a cloud moving cross him face and he wasn't looking so easy like he was looking before.

'The Babylon boys wasn't doing much, just looking at us hard and mean and walking through the crowds, slapping them batons into the palms of their hands, making us feel like we was trapped. Maybe that was when Bedward decide

105

in his mind it was now or never. The stupid old woman was still blabbering, and the Babylon boys was beating their sticks, so he had to shout out strong over the crowd, one single word. "BEHOLD!"

'Everybody quiet same time. We all look back to the saman tree. Then just like that Bedward let go of the branch he was holding. He step away from the saman tree straight out into the middle of the air.

'We hold our breath. Everybody shock. Even we who did know all along, this ability to fly without feathers. He not holding onto no branch; he not standing on anything at all, but he still up there, floating. You could tell the Babylon boys was nervous now, and the governor man who did look like a corpse before was now sweating and finally he look to me like somebody with blood running through him veins. I think to myself, never in him born days he expect to see nothing like this.

'But let me tell you something now about miracles – people get used to them real quick. The same thing that cause you mouth to drop open one minute is the same thing you take as normal the next minute. So we wait and we wait, but nothing else was happening. Bedward floating there in the middle of the air, not falling but not rising either. He just staying in the same place. Even him seem like him don't too understand. He start to scratch his head.

'The Babylon boys start to snicker, and then they start to laugh hearty as if is every day you see a man floating in the middle air. As if nothing so special in all of this. One of them shout out, "That's it! Only that? One circus trick?" And he laugh and slap his thigh.

'Bedward frowning now, and when you look real close

106

you see that he was starting to fall, little by little, coming back to earth.

'That's when Sister Gilzene come in. She who you only know now as the old woman losing her mind. Back then she was just a girl as well. Little older than me, yes – but not a grown woman yet. Still, she was the one who take matters into hand. She tell us later that all of a sudden she did remember the story of how Peter did step out onto the waves to meet the saviour, and how when he start to lose faith he did start to sink. Sister Gilzene get an understanding from this. We was losing faith. That was the problem. Even Bedward was losing faith. And we had to build it back up fast. Even in the face of Babylon, we had to build back our
faith.

'She run into the middle of the circle, stand up right under Bedward who coming down more steadily, and she close her eyes tight, lift up the palm of her hand like her faith alone could push him back into the sky. And she raise a chorus with a beautiful descant few people did even know she had inside of her. She sing, Fly away home to Zion, fly away home! Over and over, Fly away home to Zion, Fly away home!

'And now everybody get the understanding that Gilzene did get. A man cannot rise on his own. Not even a powerful man like Alexander Bedward. Him did need us. Him did need Augustown. It was we who had to push him up into the sky. It was we who had to show our faith to the govern-or and everybody else. So now all of us join in on the song, all of us raising our hands and praying. All of us hoping and believing and being people together again. All of us singing, Fly away home to Zion, fly away home!

'He start to rise again. Steadily, steadily, rising. Babylon get quiet all at once. Babylon don't have no more laugh to laugh. Babylon confounded. And now the governor man who been quiet the whole time find his voice to shout. "Get him down! Get him down!" But none of us pay him no mind. We wasn't going to let Babylon divide us again. We keep our eyes on the Master and our voices on the song.

'That is why we never see when one of them boys did run off, and we never see when him come back with a long hooker stick that people use to pick breadfruit or ackee from the tallest branch. This fellow run into the middle of the circle and just before Master could reach to a height so high as to escape the trapments of this world, that is when this fellow reach up with him long stick and hook Bedward by the neck of his robes. Catch him like him was just a ripe, ripe fruit up there to be picked. They yank the stick hard and pull the preacherman right back down to the ground.'

Ma Taffy turns her head once again to the scarred mountain. This story that she is telling was meant as a sort of distraction – to take her mind off what she does not want to know – and yet it has led her right back to the present day. *A fruit waiting to be picked*, she thinks. *The smell of jackfruit*, she thinks. *The present stench of the day.* She thinks also about how each person has a soul – and how these too are fruits that ripen every day, drawing ever closer to their harvest. And then a whole new thought. She wonders if this awful day has something to do with her own death. Perhaps. But no. If it is her own death that is to come, she wouldn't be worrying so much. That would hardly be a calamity.

She places her hand again on the butchered dome of Kaia's head. She rests it there, hoping perhaps that he will feel something of her love towards him.

'The story of Bedward,' she says, 'is not the one they been telling you. Is not the story of some fool-fool man who get it into him head that him could fly. And neither is it the story of a clumsy baff-hand man who fall out of a tree. You hearing me, child? The story of Bedward is something completely different — is the story of a man who try his best to do something big, and to reach higher than any of we did think a man like him could ever reach . . .'

The old woman pauses. She suddenly doubts the earnestness that has crept into her voice, and shrugs.

'Then again,' she continues, 'is probably just the everyday story of this goddamn island — just another striving man that this blasted country decide to pull down.'

♦

17° 59' 0" North, 76° 44' 0" West. Down there is Augustown. It sits between two hillsides, and one of these carries on its face a scar. And when these two hills throw their shadow over the valley, it can feel as if it is the dark shadow of history. Here then is the boring bit – the actual history, as it were – the things that have been recorded in official sources.

History tells us that there was once a man by the name of H. E. S. Woods, an African-American who somehow ended up in Jamaica and who was more commonly called 'Shakespeare'; the 'S' of his initials may or may not have stood for Shakespeare, the records do not say. And that this man, Shakespeare, was quite a peculiar man who lived in caves between Spanish Town and the parish of St David's, which no longer exists. And that one day in 1888, this man, Shakespeare, journeyed from St David's to Augustown and prophesied a great and terrible prophecy: *Behold*, Shakespeare said, as if he had arrived in Augustown straight from the Old Testament, *the sins of Augustown have come up before me and I will destroy this place as I did Dallas Castle, except the people repent. Yea, if they will come together, take their white cups and hold to Me a fast, I will not destroy them. But if they will not repent and obey Me, I will sink the valley and make the two hills meet.* And so the people of Augustown repented and Shakespeare made another prophecy: that a man even greater than he would rise up from that ignoble valley – that valley which from the sky looks like a great big pot of cornmeal porridge – and that this man would lead a great religion and it would be a blessing unto millions.

History says that at the time of this prophecy, Alexander Bedward was a man of little distinction; that he was a cow-herder on the nearby Mona Estate, and a gambler and an adulterer to boot. He had been afflicted with an unknown disease for many years and woke up each morning with a high fever, his broad forehead drenched with sweat and his insides feeling as if they were being turned inside out. And on such mornings he would hold his great big head in his calloused hands and bawl out, 'Oh lawd! Oh lawd! Why de raasclawt dis here sickness won't leave me be?' And then he would stumble into the yard, near to his fowl coop, and vomit until the lining of his stomach had torn and all that he was bringing up was blood. History says that the doctors were of no help to him and so he finally resolved, in the delirium of one of his fevers, to leave his wife, his girlfriends and his seven children and migrate; that he took up residence in Colon, where he worked as a labourer, and that there he suddenly enjoyed perfect health. He woke up each morning and chewed tobacco leaves, and smiled to himself and whispered, 'Foreign life good nuh, fuck!' Then, after two years, he decided to visit Jamaica, with a thick gold chain round his neck. He walked into Augustown with two packed suitcases in his calloused hands, but before reaching home he leaned the luggage against the door of a rum-bar and there he sat, well into the night, buying quart after quart of white rum so that everyone was drunk from his charity, and by the end of that night he had spent a good deal of the money he had brought back for his wife, his girlfriends and his seven children. History records that he stumbled home at last, stinking of rum, and climbed into bed beside his wife, and before she could raise her voice against him, he put his hand against her mouth and pushed himself into her; that the next morning he woke up and felt a sickness that was more than just a hangover – it was the old disease come back – and he woke up groaning *Raasclawt! Raasclawt!* and stumbled out to the fowl coop where he vomited until he saw blood. That he fainted into the mesh of the coop, scraping his face, and stayed there for hours among the feathers and the birdshit and his own vomit; that the disease refused to leave, and so he took what strength he could muster and ran away again from Jamaica.

History says that this time the disease followed him; that he was constantly delirious; that he dreamed he would die there in Panama; but that in one of his most vivid dreams he saw an old man coming out of a cave with a whip, a very peculiar man who instructed him to return at once to Augustown. That Bedward began to cry, and complained that he could not go back. He could not. He could not. *Mi naah guh back to dat raasclawt place!* But the old man flicked the whip on Bedward's back, a scoring he wore for the rest of his life; and then the man with the whip told him who he should go to and ask for money. History records that Bedward procrastinated; that the fever grew worse; that the man with the whip came to him a second time in his dream; that Bedward finally obeyed; that he got the money and returned to Jamaica and there, back on the island, he gave himself over to fasting and praying; that he cried in his wife's lap and repented; and that in the years to come he became the greatest preacherman in Jamaica. Bedwardism became one of the most important religions across the island, and for thirty years people came from all around the Caribbean to Augustown to hear this man preach. He famously said, *There is a white wall and a black wall, but the black wall is growing bigger and will crush the white wall.* He was dearly loved by the black peasants of the island, but was sorely hated by the governor and the upper-class rascals who were mostly white and who worried over his stirring oratory and the crowds he inspired. History says that he gave himself many titles; it is likely that he began as Bredda Alex, but he soon became the Shepherd and Dispenser; he was the Earl of Augustown; he was also Lord Bedward. But mostly he was Master Bedward.

History tells us that one day this one-time cowherder, former gambler and adulterer now turned preacherman, announced his intention to fly. He declared he was going to heaven to gather bolts of lightning in his calloused hands and he would bring them back down with him to that island where he would smite the white wall, the white upper-class rascals who, even though slavery had ended, were still oppressing the poor black folk. From every parish in the island and also from overseas, from Panama and from Cuba, people came; they journeyed to Augustown to see this great thing happen, and the governor was gravely worried. A group of high-powered men went into the governor's office and slammed their red fists on his Lignum vitae desk and told him, 'This cannot happen! This must not happen!' And so, on the day that Bedward was supposed to fly, the police came and arrested him. He was locked up in the madhouse, Bellevue Hospital, and he remained there for the balance of his life. History says his followers were broken by this; that the ten years in which the preacherman withered away in jail were like years in the wilderness; but that his second in command, a fellow by the name of Robert Hinds, whose story is not told enough on the island, joined forces with another man, Leonard Howell. Bedward's teachings were gathered up by these two men, mixed in with the teachings of Marcus Garvey and published in a little book called The Promised Key under the pseudonym G. G. Maragh; and you can buy this little book, even today, and this book is widely regarded as the first book of Rastafari.

You might stop to consider this: that when these dreadlocked men and women, when these children of Zion, when these smokers of weed and these singers of reggae, when they chant songs such as, 'If I had the wings of a dove', or 'I'll fly away to Zion', these songs hold within them the memory of Bedward. Such songs, sung at the right moment, can lift a man or a woman all the way up to heaven.

Call it what you will – 'history', or just another 'old-time story' – there really was a time in Jamaica, 1920 to be precise, when a great thing was about to happen but did not happen. Though people across the length and breadth of the island believed it was going to happen, though they desperately needed it to happen, it did not. But the story as it is recorded, and as it is still whispered today, is only one version. It is the story as told by people like William Grant-Stanley,

114

by journalists, by governors, by people who sat on wide verandahs overlooking the city, by people who were determined that the great thing should not happen.

Look, this isn't magic realism. This is not another story about superstitious island people and their primitive beliefs. No. You don't get off that easy. This is a story about people as real as you are, and as real as I once was before I became a bodiless thing floating up here in the sky. You may as well stop to consider a more urgent question; not whether you believe in this story or not, but whether this story is about the kinds of people you have never taken the time to believe in.

◆

This Is How It Starts

And so, I commenced the observance of fasting. Then, I began to continually see myself on the way to Augustown. Whether I slept at night or day I dreamed I was going to Augustown.

The Testimony of Mrs A. Dacosta, transcribed in 1917 by
                                                    A. A. Woods

12

To know a man properly, you must know the shape of his hurt — the specific wound around which his person has been formed like a scab. And the shape of Ian Moody's hurt is a gentleman you have already met, and who has already died. His name was Clarky.

Now if you ask him, Ian will not say that he was in love with Clarky. That would have been impossible. Ian will call down fire and brimstone and judgement on you for making such a nasty suggestion. At the time, Clarky was a big man, and he, Ian, was only a boy. And they were, neither of them, the kind who believed in that kind of love. Not even between man and woman. Love was a thing for storybooks, or for those big 'film' shows, for white people on a screen in black and white, singing their way through their simple lives. Love was for Judy Garland and Fred Astaire and Gene Kelly.

And yet . . .

From the beginning, something unspeakable had passed between them — an intensity of feeling — but the two believed in talk even less than they believed in love, which only made things worse. Unspoken, the thing between them could not dissipate. It only grew.

And what exactly drew Ian Moody to the Rastaman is also unknown. On that Thursday, the boy had spent the day outside with his sudsy pail of water. In his hand was a tattered T-shirt which he planned to wear at the end of the day but which was now being used as a washrag. His business was the washing of cars, a service he offered to customers who parked up outside Papine market. It being a Thursday meant that business was slow inside the market and even slower outside. The boy spent much of the day just sitting on the pavement, dipping his fingers in the pail of water then holding the hand above his head, letting the water drip down across his back. He enjoyed the feeling of coolness as it evaporated from his skin.

He watched fat black flies flit from one discarded fruit to another – the blighted naseberries, mangoes and pawpaws that had been left to rot in the gutter. He noticed, however, that the flies would never pitch on the discarded sections of melon, so sometimes when no one was looking he would take up one of these pieces, wash it off and eat it.

When the occasional driver turned into the parking lot and emerged from the car, Ian would spring up from the pavement and run over to make his bid.

'I clean yu car for yu, sir. Anyting yu can give.'

But always the drivers turned their faces away, pretending not to see or hear him. Ian was forced to consider the fact that he was now thirteen years old – no longer as cute as the other boys – and it made this whole thing harder. The muscles that had now begun to ripple across his body made him something of a threat.

It was midday, and another car pulled into the parking lot. Ian went over. It was a pleasingly dirty car, and someone had even fingered the words 'Wash me' on the back-glass. A thin-lipped woman emerged, clutching a purse that perfectly matched her shoes and her lipstick. These were the days when such matching was fashionable.

'Ma'am, you want me to wash the car? Anything you can give,' Ian offered.

The woman pursed her lips and observed him. He slouched, wanting to appear shorter, cuter. He smiled at her but she did not smile back.

'Why aren't you in school, young man? Your mother have you out here doing this?' she asked sternly.

Ian sucked his teeth. He wasn't in the mood for this kind of interrogation. He twisted his face as if the words were being squeezed out of it and threw his hand out extravagantly. 'Guh suck yu bloodclawt mada!' he said, and turned away from her stunned expression.

That felt good. As he walked away he tipped all the sudsy water over his body, then threw the pail with force into the gutter. He was done with that work. He walked into the market and sat across from Clarky's blue and yellow handcart. Ian had always liked Clarky. The Rastaman was kind to him. Some days he would sit across from his handcart and Clarky would peel an orange and throw it towards him. Just that. The simple things. The boy would smile and the Rastaman would nod his head.

Today, Ian watched with a new fascination the sale of these oranges, how Clarky would hold the fruit with these long, delicate fingers that suddenly didn't seem to belong to a man who sold in the market. Clarky would press the blade into the skin of the fruit and then spin it around, the skin falling away like a perfect flower; the air, for a moment, smelling of zest. He had never had a father, but today Ian thought Clarky was the kind of man he would want to become one day. Everything the Rastaman did had a strange beauty to it. He must have sat there for hours just watching. Now and again Clarky would look over to him and nod, then focus again on what he was doing – the sale of callaloo and ugli fruit and sweet, sweet oranges.

It was almost five o'clock. The market would close soon. Clarky slumped himself onto a concrete block, visibly tired. A minute later, a man stopped in front of his cart.

'Rastaman, sell me one of them orange, nuh?'

Clarky looked up at the man, and then looked across to Ian. His head didn't nod, but his eyes moved up and down to suggest a nod. Just that. Ian stood up and walked over to the cart. He took an orange from the crocus bag and then a knife to peel it. He was trembling. This felt like a test, and he could feel Clarky observing him closely. He had peeled oranges before, but Ian wanted this to be perfect. He took a breath, then slid the blade under the skin. He pressed his thumb against the raised surface of the fruit and began to spin the orange, the peel uncurling like a flower, but then he pressed too hard on the blade and pierced the flesh. A bit of juice squirted into his eyes. He frowned. Still, the skin hadn't broken. He corrected his mistake and continued to peel, the skin finally falling away. Perfect. He cut the orange in half and handed it to the man.

'Respect,' the man said, and put money into Ian's hands.

The boy walked over to hand the money to Clarky, but the Rastaman put up his hand to refuse. The boy took a seat beside him. Nothing needed to be said. Always it would be like this. They hardly ever spoke, but things were understood.

He was now the Rastaman's 'prentice', and for the next six years they worked side by side. Ian washed the handcart, arranged the produce and sometimes stood at other spots in the market, directing business towards Clarky.

And then there was one evening when he had helped Clarky push the blue and yellow handcart all the way back into Augustown. Outside his shack, Clarky had taken out a Rizla, rolled a spliff and handed it to the boy. He rolled another for himself. They had stood out there, blowing clouds of ganja into the night air. When it was late, Clarky yawned. 'Izes and protection mi yute,' he said to the boy as if to bid him goodnight, and then he turned to go into his shack. But the boy followed, and Clarky said nothing. There was only a large sponge on the floor that Clarky used as a bed. The boy disrobed himself and lay down on the sponge. Clarky did the same, unwinding the turban that was wrapped around his dreadlocks. His long hair now cascaded over his thin body. They did not touch. They fell asleep like that; though in the dark hours of the morning the boy woke up and knew that the Rastaman was awake as well. He felt his body even closer to him than before. The boy pushed his own body back slightly, and could now feel for certain that Clarky was as erect as he was. But he did not reach behind to touch the Rastaman's manhood, and soon they fell asleep again. That was as close as they had ever come to anything. And once again, without ever saying a word, Ian knew that he would never again sleep over in the Rastaman's shack. It would change things too much.

Ian had been in the market on the day the policeman had picked a fight with Clarky.

'What you have there selling, Ras?'

125

The special constable in his blue striped uniform leaned on Clarky's handcart.

Clarky's eyes fell to the floor. 'Callaloo, ugli fruit and sweet oranges, sah.'

'You sure that is all you selling, Ras? You don't have no other *vegetable matter?*' The officer grinned.

Clarky still didn't lift his eyes, but his grip tightened on the knife he was holding. 'Callaloo, ugli fruit and sweet oranges, sah,' he repeated.

The officer's grin expanded into a laugh. 'Mi don't believe you, Ras. You hiding something from me. What else you have here?' The officer thrust his hand into Clarky's cart. He began to rifle through the bunches of callaloo, as if determined to find something hidden underneath that mound of green leaves. He tossed bunches to the left and to the right. They fell on the dirty market floor.

'Bloodclawt Babylon!' Clarky shouted. He had finally lifted his eyes, but he had also lifted his hands. The blade of the knife shimmered above his head.

The officer looked at Clarky. 'But wait, Ras? Is a weapon that you have? Is assault you want to assault me?'

Clarky looked at his own hand as if both surprised and accused by it.

'No, sah!' he tried.

The officer raised his baton and swung it towards Clarky. The knife fell with a clang onto the floor.

'But is a serious crime, that, you know, Ras? Eh! A serious, serious crime.'

But Clarky's attention was once again on the callaloo. He went down on his hands and knees and began to retrieve the bunches that had been tossed out. He looked across to Ian, as if pleading for help. Ian swallowed the lump in his throat and looked away.

The officer was growing impatient. 'You goi listen to me when I talk to you, you know, Ras. You going to listen!'

Clarky was within kicking distance, and the officer did not let the opportunity pass. The Rastaman groaned when the boot made contact with his stomach and he fell, sprawled out, face down on the dirty floor.

The market erupted in noise and the youthful Ian finally found his voice.

'Why yu nuh lef de man alone?'

'De Ras touble you or something?'

'Bloodclawt police, a pussy yu a look?' Another vendor tried.

The body on the floor began to heave. The Rastaman was crying. He didn't make a sound, and yet something was pouring out from him. A thick, grey thing which was nonetheless invisible. The thing poured out of the man, and everyone in the market could feel it against their skin and in the lining of their nostrils.

The officer swung his baton a second time. A third time. A fourth time. A fifth time. The Rastaman was now being handcuffed and dragged off to jail.

A day later, Clarky walked back into Augustown without his dreadlocks, but he carried about him still this oozing, thick, grey, infectious feeling.

When Ian found out that Clarky had been released, he ran all the way to the blue and yellow shack. He stepped into the yard to find Sister Gilzene whispering, 'Saschrise! Saschrise! Jeezas Chrise!' and Ma Taffy's three nieces sobbing. Ma Taffy herself was just standing there, silent and stoic, and he wondered why they were all behaving like this when Clarky was just standing there — just standing there, without his dreadlocks, and spinning. Why was he spinning? And then the boy saw the rope. He ran back inside for one of Clarky's knives and returned to slash the rope. Clarky's lifeless body slumped into his arms, throwing him to the floor. He held onto the body of his friend for what felt like hours.

After that, Ian Moody turned fully to Rastafari. What else could he have done? What other offering could he have given to his friend but his life? He joined the bobo shantis and moved into Armagiddeon Yard — a fenced-off compound that sat on top of Dread Heights. He now calls himself Bongo Moody, and he is a man who walks around with the weight of the body that had fallen into his arms. He feels he is always carrying it with him. Clarky. That is the shape of Bongo Moody's hurt. And so the day of the autoclaps has come like a finger scratching at the scab of himself and exposing his deepest wound.

13

News of Kaia's barbering has spread like the wind. Even while the boy sits on his grandmother's verandah and listens to the story of the flying preacherman, his own story has already begun to travel as susu from every chatty-chatty mouth to every eager ear that wants to hear. It travelled even faster when he was seen walking down to Angola and then coming back with the gunman, Soft-Paw. And for everyone who gets the story, they want to be the first to have told someone else, so it goes from fence to fence and from phone to phone, circling its way around Augustown several times, so that those who were the first to deliver it will be satisfied to receive it again in just a short space of time from other sources, like a gift returned to them. Then they can say, 'Yes, man! Is just now you hearing? What a thing though, eeh man?!'

It is therefore inevitable that the story should find its way into the bobo shanti compound, but it is most unfortunate that it is the out-of-work prostitute, Doreen, who becomes the specific bearer of the news, and that it is Bongo Moody who is the one to hear it first.

Doreen had once boasted a full, healthy-bodied figure and had been one of the most sought-after whores in Augustown. Now she has become terrifyingly thin, and though no one has as yet put a name or an acronym to the disease she is obviously suffering from, men stay away, proclaiming, 'Dat gyal pussy condemn!' It is the early 1980s, and they do not realise that whatever is to be caught from Doreen has already been caught and that they are already dying a similar death to hers.

Doreen now lives her last days taking comfort and amusement in the misfortune of others. She does not appreciate that some news must be told with a tutting of the tongue, a slow shake of the head and with eyes wearily lifted to the sky. Not understanding this principle, she becomes giddy and awkward with the story of Kaia and his barbered locks. She happens to be walking by Armagiddeon Yard just as Bongo Moody is entering the compound. Across his back he carries a large string bag in which is the djembe drum he has become skilled at playing. If you hear him beat that drum he will reveal something of himself to you, for what is a drumbeat, after all, other than the sound of a great hollowness, like death amplified?

'Bongo!' she shouts after him. 'You right to keep your dreadlocks tuck safe under that turban. Next ting them hold you and chop dem off.' She laughs a keh-keh-keh laugh.

Bongo Moody observes Doreen, no small amount of annoyance in his eyes. 'Why the sistren bothering the I today?'

'Bothering? No, man. Is look I looking out for you.' Doreen laughs.

Bongo Moody shakes his head. 'All right, sistren. Blessed love.' And he makes as if to go into the compound.

Doreen panics. She has not even been given a chance to share her news. So she exclaims, 'Eh! Bongo Moody, then what? You don't hear the story? You don't know what happen in Augustown today?'

Bongo Moody pauses. He wants very much to tell this loose woman with the 'condemn pussy' that he is not one to concern himself with the trifling, everyday matters that take place in Babylon, and that furthermore he does not care to hear any susu or any carry-go-bring-come gossip from the likes of her. Yet Doreen is twitching so much and smiling so eagerly that his curiosity gets the better of him. 'All right then, my sister. What happen today?' he relents.

Doreen is ecstatic. 'You know the Rasta family that live in the house on July Street? Them is not bobo shanti like you, but them is Rasta all the same. The old woman they call Ma Taffy and the big girl she take care of, Gina?'

'Of course I know Ma Taffy!' Bongo Moody snaps. 'What? Something happen to her?'

'No. Not to her directly. But something happen to her grandson. To Miss Gina lickle boy. Look like him go school early this morning and a teacherman cut off all of the little boy hair. Yes, Bongo. The lickle boy go school with dreadlocks and come home bald as any peel-head johncrow.'

Doreen begins to laugh her ill-considered keh-keh-keh laugh. Something breaks inside Bongo Moody. It takes Doreen by surprise when the Rastaman throws his head back and shouts. 'Fyyyyyaaaaaahhhh!'

If he had just shouted it the one time she might have recovered, but he keeps on and on, like a burst pipe that cannot be plugged. 'Lawd God,' Doreen whispers. She thinks she is watching a man in the process of losing his mind. Bongo Moody draws in breath after breath, makes the barrel of his chest large, then pushes the air back out as sound: 'Fire! Fire! Fyaaah!'

He refuses to stop. The gates to Armagiddeon Yard open and the bobo shantis come out to see what is happening. Bongo Moody seems not to notice his brethren, however, and continues. It takes many calm and insistent words from the eldest of the Rastas before Bongo Moody finally quietens.

'What has disturbed the I?' the elder bobo shanti asks Bongo Moody. The elder notices Doreen and nods curtly at her. She withers under the gaze that seems to accuse her, *Whore of Babylon!*

Bongo Moody is shaking now. He tries to speak but both his eyes and voice have become moist with tears. Whatever has broken inside him has not only unleashed anger, but also sadness and a specific pain. 'Jah know! Jah know!' he keeps on saying, and nothing more. And perhaps this is right – the way he is cocooning himself in a world in which only he and his god, Jah, know and understand things. And besides, what does he really need to explain? For which of the Rastamen in front of him has not been persecuted in the same way Clarky was, or at least known someone who has been? Which one of them does not know a similar story, maybe of a Rastaman riding on his bicycle, of batons knocking him off and into the road where he bruises his body; of police searching his pockets for ganja seeds and leaves; of being thrown into jail, of having these Babylonian officers hold his head tight in the grip of their fat arms and having his locks cut off? And which of them has not listened to Babylon laughing its keh-keh-keh laugh?

Bongo Moody clears his throat and tries again to speak. He speaks slowly from his place of brokenness. 'I not a fool. I know Babylon have their tricks and evilous ways. I know what Babylon do to Jesus and Bedward and Marcus. And I know them don't respect wi Nazirite vows. I know them want to rob we of wi strength like Samson and Delilah. But Jah know, Jah know, I did think them things was in the past. I did think them things stop happen. But look like Babylon still up to the same shit.'

'My bredda,' the eldest Rastaman says to Bongo Moody. 'You right that Babylon will never change, and dem will always try to downpress the light of Rastafari. But I still don't understand what happen to the I.'

Bongo Moody looks over to the out-of-work prostitute and speaks to her. 'Tell them,' he says, as if to punish her. 'Tell them what you just tell me. Cause it look like it sweet you or something.'

Doreen shakes her head vigorously.

'Tell them!' Bongo Moody shouts.

The bobo shantis have now turned to Doreen and she looks down at the ground as if ashamed, an emotion she is not used to. She feels suddenly as if she is the one who has cut off the boy's hair. She speaks, but at least she has learnt to take the merriment out of her voice.

'You all know the elder Rasta woman who they call Ma Taffy?' she asks quietly. The bobo dreads nod. 'Well, she have a grandson, I think. Him name Kaia. It look like one teacher from the school cut off the little boy hair today. At least, that is how I hear it.'

Bongo Moody tilts his head back and goes into another fit of shouting, 'Fire!'

This time, the eldest Rastaman does not try to stop Bongo Moody. He notices, as well, the other bobos looking to him in a pleading way, their eyes telling him that this thing — this wicked thing the teacher has done to the boy — it concerns each one of them, so what are they to do? Bongo Moody's shouting finally subsides and the elder says in an almost mournful way, 'Is like Babylon want to keep we down.'

'That's why Rasta must stand up to Babylon,' says Ras Benedict dangerously. He is an ex-convict who found the light of Rasta while in prison, but everything he says still has a certain menace about it, and even the other bobo dreads are a little afraid of him.

'March!' a younger bobo shouts, wanting to be part of this excitement. The word lingers in the air. They all seem to contemplate it. Life, of course, is often shaped by such things – the word that is not only said, but that lingers; the sentence that is not only spoken, but pronounced – these syllables that stick in the air until everyone feels their stickiness, these syllables that grow out from a mere utterance into something tangible, like the woman who turns to her husband one morning and says, 'It's over,' or the field slave who whispers to the stalk of cane he is about to cut a simple word: 'freedom'. A march? The word sticks. No one can find an objection. The bobo shantis go back into Armagiddeon Yard to retrieve their flags and then, just like that, they proceed to march through Augustown. And this is how it starts.

14

Augustown has rhythms and patterns from which is constructed its own sense of the banal, of the unspectacular, of the 'hardly to be commented on'. For this reason not even the three-legged dog, Cocoa – who eats out of the garbage bins he religiously overturns and who sleeps so soundly in a pothole each night that cars have to honk their horns or flash their bright lights and wait for the mutt to yawn and, in his slow, limping way, extract himself from the cracked depression in the road – raises a single eyebrow. And neither has anyone commented incredulously on the occasional sighting of Miss Katie in her backyard picking naseberries from her tree, stark naked, the fold of her belly hanging so low that it actually covers her nether parts. As well, the occasional death of a rudeboy from gunshot wounds might be remarked on for a day or two, but never longer than that. Such events, having been carefully weighed and considered, will be dismissed as banal.

And yet it is also true that from the time of the flying preacherman to now, Augustown has become a place that fully expects the extraordinary. Every day they wait on it, and when it comes they greet it with what might seem to the undiscerning eye to be the same amount of indifference with which they greet the ordinary. And indeed it is indifference, but of a different kind, their bodies relaxing into the new events as if this, at last, is the life they have always been meant to live.

The march of the bobo shantis falls well outside the regular rhythms and patterns of Augustown. It breaks the monotony of things, and will live on in the collective memory as a happening as strange as it is spectacular.

The procession is first seen coming down from Dread Heights. Word goes round fast: *The bobo dreads marching! The bobo dreads marching!* All over Augustown there is the rattling of latches being unbolted and windows and doors and shutters being flung open. People either look out or go into the streets to see the bobo shantis pass.

When the initial excitement evaporates, it is replaced by something even stronger – a sense of awe. The bobo shantis are not making a sound. No chanting, no singing, no nothing. There is something in this solemnity that humbles everyone, something beautiful and terrifying. The bobo shantis wear long beards and priestly gowns. Around their necks are draped shawls in the colours of Ethiopia – red, green and gold. Their dreadlocks are piled on top of their heads and then hidden under tight turbans which rise towards the sky. The procession looks like something from Egypt – like a delegation of high priests on their way to meet Pharaoh. The bobo dreads are carrying banners as well – flags, again in the colours of Ethiopia, or with drawings of the Lion of Judah on them.

The procession begins to grow. People come out not only to see, but to join in. They leave their houses, their yards, the street corners on which they are idling, and one by one they file in behind the bobo dreads. Some people join as a sort of joke, but as soon as they are marching they lift their heads high with a stern sense of purpose. It soon becomes a procession of barefoot children, of women in bathroom slippers with curlers still in their hair, of baldheads, of Christians, of backsliders. The march of the bobo shantis becomes the march of Augustown – another inching, another 'trodding' towards some place they have been trying to reach for over a hundred and fifty years.

They have marched before, of course. On 1 August 1838 – what they now call 'August Morning' – they had packed massive hampers onto their heads and marched straight off the Mona and Papine Estates, knowing that this time Massa could not send his dogs to chase them. Queen Victoria had signed the paper that gave them back their freedom. Their feet felt strange with this knowledge that they could go wherever they wanted to go, though some of the old people said that where they really wanted to go was across the large sea, and for that they would have needed wings.

They did not march far: less than a mile, to this valley. They called it Augustown, as if the place itself were the freedom they had just received, but time would teach them disappointment. This place was no freedom, and Massa Day was not done. Massa had only changed his name. He was no longer 'Busha' or 'Buckra' or 'Massa'. He was now 'Boss' or 'Miss' or 'Sergeant'. Sometimes Massa even changed his skin from white to black, making this whole freedom thing complicated. There was further to go; a longer journey ahead.

And so they have marched many more times since August Morning. They have joined every workers' strike, been part of every vigil and every rally, but no march has ever got them to the place they want to reach. Yet they continue, with an almost Sisyphean resolve. They have decided that if they cannot accomplish a mile, then maybe they can accomplish a yard or even an inch. If they cannot accomplish the destination, then at least they will pull closer, closer with every opportunity that presents itself. They will inch slowly towards this elusive place – step by step, lickle bi lickle. They bank their faith in proverbs. They say, *Stone by stone de wall fall.* Or, *Every dog have him day and every puss him four o'clock.* Or, *Every day devil help tief but one day God a guh help de watchman.* And so they march, waiting for their Jericho, for the wall to fall, waiting for their four o'clock, waiting for the Day of the Watchman. And when Augustown sees the bobo shantis, they cannot resist the solemnity of it all, those flags unfurling, the Lions of Judah rippling into life as if at any moment, if the breeze were just strong enough, they might just throw their heads back, leap off of the fabric and roar.

One by one the residents of Augustown file in behind the bobo shantis, their heads held high, marching with an uprightness that can be traced back to that very first march, as if even now there are still large hampers on top of their heads.

They walk from August Road up to July Street, then across to Patterson Road, then John Golding Road. With every step the crowd grows larger. A sharp left onto Silvera Road. Then down, and then up, then down again. They are going towards a destination as yet unspoken. But of course, it is the school.

The teaching day now done, the campus all but empty, rumour has it that the wicked teacher is still there. So the school pulses, a terrible darkness in the middle of Augustown, pulling the marchers towards its awful centre.

Augustown Primary looks like almost every other primary school on the island, which is to say that despite its blue-and pink-painted buildings, despite what is supposed to be a sort of pastel innocence, it wears a stern expression. On most days this sternness gives reassurance to passers-by, Jamaican parents who do not see fit to send their children to places where anything so flippant as fun might be encouraged. Behind the chain-link fence is not a prison, exactly, but a pleasingly close relation. Today, the lack of swings and sandpits and jungle gyms serves another function, however: not to give assurance to would-be parents, but to lend gravitas to the crowd that will soon gather before it. Augustown Primary has become the site of Babylon.

This is not the most organised march in the history of Augustown. The crowd has not made placards, and there is no news camera for them to perform to. Someone picks up a stone and throws it at the closed gate. It bounces off the chain-link fence but causes a clanging sound.

'Weh de teacherman deh?' someone shouts. 'Where him is? We want justice!'

'Justice!' someone else shouts. 'A fuckery ting dem do to the little yute.'

'Send him out here! Send out the teacherman!'

Bongo Moody seems to have a greater sense of purpose. He positions himself directly in front of the school gate and pulls his djembe drum out of its bag. His hands begin to fall lightly on the goatskinned instrument, and he pulls the crowd into the hollow of its sound. He has a fine singing voice, and he makes it ring out over the schoolyard.

> *Hear the words of the Rastaman say*
> *Babylon yu throne gone down, gone down*
> *Babylon yu throne gone down . . .*

The air feels like death. The sun dips behind a cloud and a coolness that could be rain but that isn't rain sweeps over the landscape. Bongo Moody plays and the crowd sings behind him.

In classroom 2B, Mr Saint-Josephs, still at his desk, listens. Tears begin to stream down his face. He has never been an emotional man, but he knows that this is about him. It is about the terrible thing he has done. He realises now that it was not the principal he should have prepared himself for; it is this. He has called the Rastas down on him – this tribe of hooligans. He feels every clap of the drum in his bones, each one like a prophecy of his doom.

On her verandah, Ma Taffy is also listening. She begins to tremble. Kaia runs out into the road, looking to his left and his right. If he had thought to ask his grandmother, she would have told him where the sound was coming from. 'The school. It is coming from the school.' But Kaia is also interested in something else.

'Grandma!' he calls to her. 'Is the same song you was just telling me about. Don't it? Is the same song!' He turns back, only to realise that Ma Taffy's trembling has taken her all the way down to the floor. She too has fresh tears running down her face. Ma Taffy thinks, *The jackfruit is falling; the rats dem raining from the roof; the autoclaps start for true. Whatever going to happen, it happening now.*

And then they hear it: another voice, right alongside the drumbeat, but even louder. This new voice is coming from somewhere else, somewhere at once closer and much further away. From a house close by, but also from the past. It is a beautiful soprano, almost birdlike, but it swells . . .

> *Fly away home to Zion, fly away home!*
> *One bright morning when man work is over*
> *Man will fly away home.*

15

If Augustown has rhythms and patterns, so too does the woman whose job it is each evening to sweep and mop out the classrooms at Augustown Primary, and then arrange the chairs and desks in a neat way. She is not a woman entirely in her right mind. At best, you might say she is a functional schizophrenic, and that employment as ancillary staff at the school suits her disposition perfectly. There is something about the monotony of sweeping and mopping that lends a stable rhythm to her being; something about the ordering of desks and chairs that seems to order her mind, if only just a little. And because the school is practically empty while she works, she does not have to strain to silence the voices in her head; she can give them free rein. And nor does she have to resist the urge to talk back to them. As she cleans the classrooms, an oily red bandana tied around her head, she carries on animated conversations with her long-dead mother and father, with her brothers and sisters, with her dog, with aliens and sometimes with CIA agents; with Bob Marley, Patti LaBelle, or with the Prime Minister.

On this day of the autoclaps, the cleaning lady has been scolding her dog, Jack Sprat, who, thirty years earlier, had found and eaten the salt mackerel her mother had put up carefully. Her addled mind has made the long-ago incident suddenly current, and as she goes from classroom to classroom, her eyes glued to the dirty floor while she sweeps and mops, the cleaning lady thoroughly lambasts the worthless mongrel.

'So what? You tink you is smaddy? Eh? You tink you can just eat off people mackerel like say you is a big person? Listen to me nuh, dawg, don't make I kill you in here today. What you tink dis is? And don't you grin off you face at me neither. You think is joke I making? Eh?'

When she enters classroom 2B, the shouting and the drumming and the singing have only just started outside the gate. It annoys her, for this is not the rhythm that she works to. She tries to block it out. She focuses on her dog, and on her broom, and on the floor she has to clean, so at first she does not notice Mr Saint-Josephs still sitting by his desk. She sweeps the floor while reprimanding the phantom dog. It is only when her broom reaches what seems to be a long black cotton snake that she pauses. She looks carefully at the thing, at the wisps of hair spiralling out from it. It is a dreadlock. She has never seen one detached from a head. And there are more beside it. It is only now that she looks up and sees Mr Saint-Josephs sitting there like some kind of zombie, the only sign of life being tears running down his broad face. The woman is so frightened she almost screams. It has taken her a while to see him, but he seems still not to have noticed her.

'Sir?' she tries.

He does not respond.

'Hello?'

He raises a feeble hand as if to say hello, or else to shoo

143

away a fly, and then he puts it back down.

'Sir? You not going home today?' She is even more annoyed now. Why should he still be here, interrupting her cleaning?

Mr Saint-Josephs shakes his head. After a moment he mutters, 'Trelawny too far. And the buses stop run.'

But the man lives in Mona. The cleaning lady knows this. She spins around, wondering if someone is playing a joke on her, or if she is being watched again – spied on, as she often decides she is. There is no one else around but Jack Sprat, who is wagging his tail while sniffing at the dreadlocks on the floor.

'Come, Jack! Come!' the cleaning lady hisses, and with the certain instinct that preserves life, even of the crazy, she slowly retreats out of the classroom. She does not go far, though. She cleans the other classrooms nearby and then waits patiently in the shadows for Mr Saint-Josephs to leave.

The great philosophical question goes: if a tree falls in a forest and no one is around to hear, does it make a sound? But this is a troubling question, exalting one kind of being above all others. What then of the ears of snakes, or wood frogs, or mice, or bugs? Do they not count? What then of grass, of stone, of earth? Does their witness not matter? If a man flies in Jamaica, and only the poor will admit to seeing it, has he still flown?

The cleaning woman waits. Every now and then she peeks into the classroom. She is waiting for the teacher to leave, but also – unknown even to her – she is waiting, as he is, for something else.

Always – always – there are witnesses.

144

16

About an hour or so before she dies, a feeling, like that of being lowered into cool river water, comes over Sister Gilzene. Where she was ranting and cursing only minutes before, she now experiences a kind of peace, and her mind finds its right and proper order. She swings her feet around and rises up out of the bed she has been virtually trapped in for months. Strange, she thinks. She lifts a frail hand to her chest and opens her mouth to make the long sound, *aaaaaaaah*. She opens her mouth again and makes the sound *ooooooh*. She nods to herself. It has come back to her – her voice. All the croaking, creaking and rattling of old age have fallen away from her vocal chords, just like that, and she has it again: the sweet, pure descant that used to bring many a heathen to church. And then she understands with absolute certainty that this is how it ends; that she is about to die, but also, that she is supposed to leave behind her a song. As yet she does not know which song, but she supposes this will come to her in time.

She walks over to the window and pulls back the thin lace curtain to look out upon Augustown for one last time. How things have changed over the years! Most of the wooden houses have been torn down and replaced by concrete structures as small and as hot as ovens. And the oven-houses are not painted, so they still have the green-brown colour of wet cement. The skyline is now a crowd of black wires stretched between evenly spaced poles. It is the poles which look most peculiar to Sister Gilzene – like a line of crucifixion crosses, Calvary repeating and repeating itself along every road.

There is a sound behind her. She turns around to see the surprised face of the little girl from next door, whose mother sends her over each afternoon to make sure the old woman is all right. Always the little girl seems to resent this simple task and will never linger. She usually just looks in from the doorway and shouts to her mother, 'She still just lie dung inna di bed. She naah move or nothing,' and then she slams the door and runs off, presumably to do the more important things that little children have to do. Today, however, she is all eyes and gaping mouth. When she was a younger woman, Sister Gilzene was used to people staring at her. Her features were striking, from the deep black of her skin, to her high forehead, to her eyes, which were neither wide nor squinty but which seemed rectangular, like a goat's; indeed her entire face seemed to have in it more bone than any other. People would be struck by this combination of features, the strength of Gilzene's look; they would scrutinise her for a moment or two, and then – though it was never their first thought – they would inevitably arrive at the conclusion that she was striking but ugly, or that she was ugly, but in an interesting way. Old age, however, has robbed Gilzene of her striking looks; with her wrinkles and grey hair, she looks like every other old woman and has forgotten what it feels like to be stared at.

146

'Let we call it a second wind,' Sister Gilzene offers the girl by way of explanation. 'Don't worry. It won't last long. I soon dead.'

The little girl gasps, surprised not by the statement itself, but by the strength in that usually ragged voice. But she is a brave girl, and instead of running away she steps further into the room, closer to Sister Gilzene, and looks the old woman up and down.

'What wrong?' Sister Gilzene asks, growing a little annoyed at the intrusion.

The girl thinks about this. What is wrong? Everything is wrong! Nothing has been right about the day, and yet it occurs to her that wrong days are so much more exciting than 'right' days. 'Plenty things wrong,' the little girl says brightly. 'Like one madniss fly up inna Mr Saint-Josephs' head today and him go chop off Kaia dreadlocks in class. Now everybody talking bout it, and I hear seh all the bobo dread dem from Armagiddeon Yard gone marching to the school.'

'Is that so?' Sister Gilzene asks, genuinely curious. Surely this has something to do with the song she is supposed to leave behind.

'Yes, ma'am,' the girl confirms. 'That is where I was going. Everybody gone down there with them. Is just that Mama say I must come here first.'

'I see,' says Sister Gilzene, turning back to the window and pulling the curtain. Yes . . . she can feel the relative emptiness of the streets, but also a sort of tension. A crowd is definitely gathering somewhere. 'You can go now, little girl.' She calls behind her. 'Tell you mada thanks, and that me is all right.'

After a minute, she realises she has not heard the door

close. She looks behind her and sees the little girl is still there.

'What now?' Sister Gilzene asks.

The little girl turns her two palms up and shrugs her shoulders, but stands resolutely. The sight of an invalid old woman who has risen out of her bed is now more of a spectacle to her than the procession that has made its way to the school.

Sister Gilzene sighs. She will not get rid of the girl so easily and she knows it. She walks over to a chair and sits down. If the girl is going to stay, then so be it. She may be of some use after all.

'Every day you come over here and look pon me in mi bed, and me don't even know yu name. What dem call yu?'

'Lloydisha dem call mi, ma'am.'

'Lloydisha?' the old woman repeats, and laughs a little. 'Them getting creative with these names!'

The little girl scowls at the old woman.

'Awrite, awrite,' Sister Gilzene says. 'Don't vex with me. Is a nice name.' But she is still smiling to herself.

'Mi fada name Lloyd,' the girl explains.

'Yes, I think everybody who hear yu name will know that.' Sister Gilzene chuckles again. She takes a deep breath and considers the girl. 'Lloydisha, you know me is a very old woman, and that me soon going to dead?'

'Yes, ma'am,' Lloydisha says, 'everybody know. Every day mi fada ask mi mada if you don't dead yet.'

Sister Gilzene chuckles again. 'By day's end, for sure.'

'Day's end, ma'am?' Lloydisha asks, screwing up her face.

'Yes,' Sister Gilzene answers, though she is sure the child

does not understand her full meaning. 'You know what going to happen when I dead?'

'Yes, ma'am. Dem going to put you into one hole. Then Mama and Papa will get this room.'

'I suppose so. Yes. But it won't just be me alone down there in that hole.'

'Why? Somebody else going to dead?'

Years later, Lloydisha will wonder if she really had asked this question, and she will shiver when she thinks of how prophetic it turned out to be. Sister Gilzene, however, is not gifted in such a way. She cannot see the future beyond her own death, so she answers, 'No. Nobody else going to dead. But you best believe that other things goi be down there in that hole. Some things that should be there, like worms. And other things that shouldn't be there. Like old-time stories. Like history.'

'History?' Lloydisha asks, her voice full of disbelief.

Sister Gilzene nods. 'Of course. Every time a person dead, a part of history go and dead with them too. Well . . . unless . . .'

Lloydisha wrings her hands and skips from foot to foot waiting on the old woman to finish the sentence. 'Unless what?' she almost shouts.

Sister Gilzene fixes her eyes on the girl, and then she lifts her chin slowly as if to measure the girl's adequacy.

Lloydisha understands that she is being assessed, and she stands up straight with her hands at her sides, hoping to be found worthy.

At last Sister Gilzene nods. Her inspection is complete. 'You want to hear a story?'

'Ma'am?'

'I ask if you want to hear a story. Maybe you can keep it for me, and keep it from the hole where they going to bury me soon. But you cannot be selfish with it, Lloydisha. If I tell you, you have to make sure it don't die with you either.'

Lloydisha feels her head swelling, and decides that this is definitely more interesting than the march of the bobo shantis. She nods her head vigorously, up and down, up and down.

'Awrite then.' Sister Gilzene turns her head towards the curtain that is now closed and begins to speak. 'Long time ago there was a man right here in Augustown, and when I think bout it now, maybe him was the first prophet of Rastafari. But back then nobody was Rasta. Back then we was Bedwardites.'

'You talking bout Marcus Garvey?' Lloydisha asks quizzically. There are so many Rastas in Augustown and she has heard them talking and reasoning about the prophet, but the name she knows is Marcus Garvey.

Sister Gilzene smiles. 'Yes. I suppose that is what people will tell you, but that is not the man I talking bout right now. I talking bout another fellow. His name was Alexander Bedward, and him did have a church right here in Augustown. They call it Union Camp – a church for poor people, but them did build it as big as any Great House. As big as a hospital, so you can imagine Babylon was fraid of this church. Every Sunday we used to pack up in Union Camp to hear this preacherman preach. Him was a very special man. Yes . . . Garvey tell we to look out for a black king, but is Bedward who did learn we bout Zion. Is Bedward who tell we to farm the land and grow we own crops. Is

Bedward who tell we to give up salt pork and salt fish, cause salt is a thing that weigh black people down from their flying destiny. You have to understand this, little girl. This man I telling you about, is almost like he did have wings. Oh yes, my dear. Mmm-hm. This preacherman could fly.'

The old woman tells her story and the little girl, Lloydisha, listens. Then, when she is finished, Sister Gilzene gets up and goes over to the window and parts the curtains again. As she does this, the clear sound of a drumbeat comes to her. It is playing somewhere in the distance, but it is a song she already knows. She puts a frail hand on her chest, opens her mouth and then releases the incredible thing, the thing that makes everyone for miles around hold their breath: the beautiful descant that makes the crowd at the school spin to their left and to their right; the song that makes Ma Taffy sprawl out weeping on her verandah; the thing that makes Miss G and Mrs G strain their eyes from Beverly Hills towards Augustown.

Afterwards, everything is quiet. It is so quiet that those nearby might even have heard the gentle thud of the old woman falling to the ground and her small bones breaking. It is not the way death is supposed to happen. There is no wind; no dogs are barking; no cocks are crowing. The drumming and singing down by Augustown Primary has paused. Even the radio host, Mutty Perkins, seems to have fallen into an uncharacteristic silence.

It is the little girl, Lloydisha, who brings everyone back to themselves. She runs out into the streets and shouts, 'She drop dung and dead! The old woman dis drop dung and dead!'

Ten days from now the old woman will be buried in Bedward Cemetery. Her tombstone will read: Gilzene Beatrice Philips, Songstress, 28 September 1905–11 April 1982. And hers is the first death on the day of the autoclaps.

The Autoclaps

Da one ya name Attaclaps,
Babylon a guh collapse.
Jah know mi really haffi grow mi locks
Da one ya a de Attaclaps, Attaclaps!
Thunder roll and more lightning flash.

Sizzla Kalonji

♦

Down there is Augustown, and you could say it is a place that has been rocked by one autoclaps after another, rolling over the valley like hurricanes. A strange word, autoclaps. And I have not explained it to you. It is not the kind of word you will find in the Oxford dictionary. But maybe if you were lucky enough to find a dictionary that had in it blackpeople's words, then the entry for 'autoclaps' would read something like this:

> **Autoclaps:** (Noun). Jamaican dialect. *An impending disaster; Calamity; Trouble on top of trouble.* Variously pronounced 'attaclaps', or (given the Jamaican tendency to add 'H's in front of vowels) 'hattaclaps'.

The etymology is disputed. One person will tell you that it

comes from autocollapse, but I think this is unlikely. The word 'autocollapse' is a new coinage, while the word 'auto-claps' has been whispered throughout the Caribbean for a few hundred years at least. *Lawd chile! Massa catch him trying to run away, and the whip fall pon him back like an autoclaps!*

Another person will tell you that the word means, quite literally, heart collapse. This is unlikely too, but maybe it inches us closer to the truth. After all, what else is an auto-claps but that moment when the heart rises up, up, up from the chest, then gets stuck in the mouth, a thick red sponge that we gag on? What else is an autoclaps but that moment when the heart fails – that moment, coming soon, when Ma Taffy will run from her verandah and into the street, will fall to her knees wanting to shout, *Stop! Stop! Stop!* But her heart! Her useless, useless heart, like a stifling sponge in her mouth.

Most Jamaicans, however, will tell you this – that the word 'autoclaps' comes to us from the Bible; that it is a cre-ole derivative of 'Apocalypse'. Apocalypse, originally Greek. Apokalypsis: *a disclosure; an uncovering of knowledge.* That word lost its original meaning somewhere in the twelfth century, stopped meaning a general revelation and came to mean a specific one as found in the Book of Revelation: the end of the world and of all mankind. The theory goes that even as the word travelled through time and space and localised itself in the tropical Caribbean, so too did the disaster it prophesied become localised. An autoclaps is not quite the same as an apocalypse. An autoclaps does not come with four horsemen or seven trumpets or seven seals or any of the other things you might have read about in the Bible. An autoclaps does not mean the end of all time, nor the end of

158

all humanity – though it might very well mean the end of one life. Possibly two.

But, see, here is the thing: even this last explanation, by far the most popular, is actually incorrect. The word did not come to Jamaica via the Bible, but from a word belonging to fourteenth-century English dialect – Afterclap.

> **Afterclap:** Noun. *An unexpected, often un-pleasant sequel to a matter that had been consid-ered closed.* In German, 'achterklap'.

It's funny, isn't it, this whole process – how various dialects bleed into each other; how every language is a graveyard of languages, how every language is a storehouse of history. But what does it all matter, this useless fretting over the beginnings of a word? Autoclaps. The fact is, the word exists. Even to say it causes a sense of dread. And all these various meanings bear their weights down onto the word.

> **Autoclaps:** the collapse of the heart; a small apocalypse; the afterclap.

◆

17

From certain points in Beverly Hills, a man can stand under the shade of a sweet almond tree, or sit on a piece of limestone that juts out from the earth like a warped tooth, and observe the island that spreads itself out like an apron around him. His vantage point might even be comparable to ours up here in the sky. There are three elevations for him to observe.

The highest is, of course, where he is – Beverly Hills itself. You would be forgiven for thinking, at first, that this affluent hilltop suburb of the West Indies had borrowed its name from that other famously affluent city in California, but this is not the case. The first developer that went in, dynamiting the limestone and laying down foundations for grand houses on the hillside, had simply named the place after his wife. Still, the houses of Beverly Hills, Jamaica are just as impressive as those of Beverly Hills, California. Most of them are spread over three or four floors and they perch in such a way as to flaunt their daring architecture. These are not the kinds of houses to tuck themselves away in the landscape, or to hide behind a sprawl of bamboo, as they might in other parts of Jamaica such as Irish Town. The fences surrounding the mansions of Beverly Hills are therefore tall and topped with electric wire. There are often guardhouses at the front and pools round the back. Perhaps there is too much effort in all of this, too much aspiration, but the houses seem rather pleased with themselves and look down with contempt on all that lies below.

Right below Beverly Hills, there on the flats, is yet another suburb, this one going by the name of Mona. Mona was once a neat community, but today many of its bungalows have grown untidily into two-storey houses, guts of concrete blocks and cement spilling into the small yard spaces. The fences surrounding these units, however, remain low enough for neighbours to be able to talk to each other in the evenings while watering their garden or washing their car. The streets of Mona are named after flowers: Daisy Avenue, Plumbago Path, Carnation Way, and so on. One exception is Mona Road itself. You can come to it from the foot of Beverly Hills, turning onto Munro Road, which becomes Wellington Drive, which delivers you onto Mona Road, a long thoroughfare that runs straight and sure all the way through Mona and then beyond.

And were the man to follow the full length of this road with his eyes, past the old aqueduct that once watered the sugar plantations of the area, past the Mona Reservoir with its constant flock of egrets perched on the perimeter and looking into the dark water – these white birds that old people insist are the spirits of the dead – past the sprawling, occasionally green, occasionally brown-grassed campus of the University of the West Indies; were he to take it until it declines in both angle and quality, until potholes adorn both sides of the road, making it a kind of obstacle course, follow it until the road ups and changes its name from Mona to John Golding, then he would now be observing the third level, the lowest elevation, a dismal little valley on a dismal little island. Augustown.

And if such a man were still viewing all of this from the safe vantage point of Beverly Hills, under the shade of that sweet almond tree, and now with the necessary aid of a pair of binoculars, then the ramshackle valley might look something like a pot of cornmeal porridge, rusting tin roofs stirred into its hot, bubbling vortex.

And with his binoculars he might occasionally see a resident of Augustown looking up to where he is standing. He might even feel a little afraid. What irony, this sudden panic of being watched, this feeling that the affluent community in which he finds himself is somehow threatened by this other person he has been observing all along – a lone woman, perhaps, who, in looking up, must feel the unfair weight of all that privilege rising above her.

In many ways, Mrs G is a typical resident of Beverly Hills; which is to say, she is a fair-skinned woman – almost white – who lives in a large house with her wealthy husband. It is a wide and airy house full of paintings and sculptures. Mrs G has a fine eye for art. On the white wall, the academic realism of Barrington Watson hangs beside the less measured but more joyful brushstrokes of Ken Spencer and the religious iconography of Oswald Watson. She even has an original Carl Abrahams and two drawings by Edna Manley. But the house is also full of books, and perhaps this is the first thing – this voracious reading – that makes Mrs G not typical at all. Whenever she casts her eyes down to Mona, and then towards Augustown, she is overcome with several emotions, but none of them is fear. Mrs G loves Augustown, and in fact has a relationship with it. Every weekday morning, and sometimes on Saturdays as well, she gets behind the wheel of her blue Honda Accord and drives the twelve-minute drive down the hill, through Mona and then on towards the troubled community where she is principal of the primary school.

In her office, she often spends time looking through the louvred windows at the schoolyard and the children in their uniform. This creates an ache in her heart. The principalship is not a job she had wanted, and now that she has it, it is not a job that she likes. For the fifteen years before she was made principal, she had been the most successful teacher at Augustown Primary. She misses it.

Her small office is never tidy. It is an extension of the library at her house. The shelves are bursting with books and papers: every journal, every study, every report on educational matters that she has been able to get her hands on is here. There is no art on the walls here – just her certificates. A first degree in literature, a master's degree in early childhood education and another master's degree in social work. The teachers who come to her office resent this a little, but none more so than Miss Sterling, the vice principal, who was passed over for the top job. Everyone knows that Miss Sterling is undereducated and incompetent, but it does not matter. She is, after all, a serious church woman. Miss Sterling it is who spends many evenings taking random buses throughout Kingston, giving sermons. Because of the sternness of her character and the quality of righteousness that emanates from her, the other teachers have meekly accepted her de facto leadership and have joined her in resenting the almost-white woman who has now become their principal. They do not know that Mrs G would give anything to trade places with them.

The job of vice principal had come up more than once, and had been presented to Mrs G as a sort of gift, as something she should have been pleased about. But she had turned these opportunities down. She wasn't in this profession for prestige or money. Teaching was her calling, and she didn't want to leave it for the drudgery of administration. But when the long-serving principal finally came to retire, she pressed heavily on Mrs G to take over.

'I really don't know what to do,' Mrs G had said to her husband one evening.

Mr Garrick, a carpet of grey hair spread over the wide girth of his belly, and his belly folded over the rim of his silk boxer shorts, observed his wife's quivering lips and was touched again by how vulnerable she could be. He understood the simple thing that she wanted from him: she needed his understanding, almost his permission to turn down this new offer. Mr Garrick felt cruel that he could not give this to her.

Mr Garrick was a selfish man. He did not give to charities; he had never donated any work of art to the National Gallery; he did not sit on any national board. Though he was a white Jamaican man, and though he was now wealthy, he hadn't been born into it, and so all his life he had worked hard to acquire the wealth people naturally assumed he had always possessed because of his colour. Relentlessly ambitious, he had often felt ashamed of his wife's position – a mere teacher, and at a primary school to boot, and in a ghetto, as if to add insult to his deep and abiding sense of injury. He would

164

have preferred it if she were just a housewife, and had even suggested it, but with catastrophic results that ended up with him sleeping in the spare bedroom for two nights. 'Principal', however! That had a much better ring to it.

'Apply for the damned thing, Claudia. Tell me one good reason why you wouldn't. All those books you reading day in and day out, all those conferences you been been going to . . . you can finally put it all to some use!'

'Oh, Timothy, for godsake, I put it to use every day in my classes. Every day!'

'You know what I mean, Claudia. I'm talking about policy here. Policies are how things change. Take it from me. If you're in charge of policy, you can make a lot more difference than you would in just one classroom.'

Mrs G bit her lip and turned away. Timothy Garrick softened a little and reached for her hand. 'Think about it, Claudia. You could do something great.'

So Mrs G had applied for the job, hoping that she would not get it but knowing that she would. Her husband's promise has turned out to be untrue, for in the five years that she has been doing this job she has not got around to doing anything 'great'. There are too many everyday things that get in the way of greatness: canteen staff and groundsmen and ancillary workers to supervise; reports to send off to the Ministry of Education; inspections around the school to conduct; water bills and light bills and phone bills to pay; interviews to conduct; replacement teachers to hire. She has tried to formulate new policies, but the staff ignore them. She has organised workshops on Saturdays but the staff do not attend.

Still, it is the teaching that Mrs G misses more than

anything; it is her absence from the classroom that makes her depressed, and this is why she has embarked on her strangest and most ambitious project yet. Each evening, back at her large house in Beverly Hills, she has been giving lessons to her domestic helper, Miss G. Now, do not be confused. In this house there is Mrs G, the boss and teacher, and Miss G, the helper and student. But all of this ended on the day of the autoclaps.

18

About three years earlier, Mrs G had woken from sleep with a knowing lodged somewhere beneath her ribcage. The knowing was painful. It felt like an uncomfortable mass pressing against her insides. She had kept her eyes closed, trying to fall back asleep, trying to dream, trying not to know the thing that she suddenly knew. She squirmed in the bed and frowned.

'Sorry, darling, I didn't mean to wake you,' Timothy apologised. He had just lifted himself carefully out of the bed.

Mrs G grunted, but it wasn't him that had woken her; it was this sudden knowing. She waited for her husband to get ready as he always did early on a Wednesday morning, packing his work clothes into a bag then driving himself to Liguanea Club for a squash game before heading to work.

'I'll see you later this evening,' Timothy said as he left the room, turning the lights off.

Mrs G grunted again and tried once more to fall asleep, but sleep would not come. Instead, she thought about the various tasks she had to do that day. She thought about them in great detail. When that did not work, she thought about her son, who was doing so well at college. How very proud she was of the boy! Finishing up his first degree and jumping straight into a PhD programme. She pictured him in her mind and tried to let the warm feelings of mother-hood wash over her. But no. The knowing was still there. She knew, she knew. Goddammit. She knew. She hissed, and finally hauled herself out of bed. She pulled on her robe and proceeded to walk around the house, checking the cupboards and all the drawers, doing a careful inventory of things. Missing were three of her blouses, four pairs of her shoes, her favourite silver necklace, at least half a dozen of Timothy's T-shirts, two of his work shirts and a small AM/FM radio that was usually kept in the kitchen. With this small loot gone, the knowing that had woken her up was confirmed. She would never again see Miss Liza, the house-keeper who last Friday had gone home to Clarendon for the weekend and who should have returned bright and early on Monday morning. But now it was Wednesday, and Miss Liza was nowhere to be seen. Miss Liza had worked at the house for all of three weeks and had even come with high recommendations.

Mrs Martin, who managed the canteen at Augustown Pri-mary, had said, 'Mrs G, I hear you having no luck finding a helper. What a shame, eeh man?! Terrible shame. It hard to find honest people, Mrs G. I know how it go. Well, ma'am, in case you still in need, I have a cousin, you see – Liza she name. Come from country. Yes, ma'am, country she come from, so you know she not like them tiefing Kingston gyal who will tief all the milk from your coffee. Yes, ma'am. Liza is a nice Christian girl from Clarendon and she have clean ways. She will wash and cook and clean if that is what you need. So I just saying, if you still looking for somebody, I can send her your way. Poor thing. She fall on hard times recently, Mrs G, and just looking for a little work. No hand-out. Just a little work.'

So Miss Liza had arrived three weeks ago, and now Miss Liza was gone. In total, Mrs G had seen five helpers come and go over the last three months, and the things they had stolen from around the house added up to more than she could be bothered to count.

Mrs G pulled her robe around her, sat down at her dining table and placed her head in the cup of her hands. 'Oh Blanche, Blanche, Blanche,' she moaned, incanting the name of the woman who had worked with the Garricks faithfully for fifteen years. But Blanche had recently been sent for, moving all the way to America to be with an ageing sister, and now Mrs G was at a loss as to how to replace her.

Mrs G had been sitting in the same position for a while, nodding off occasionally into a shallow sleep. But then she had heard a sound from outside. 'Hello? Hello?' Had Miss Liza really returned? The call was followed by a pinging at the gate.

Mrs G walked over to the kitchen door and peered out, but it wasn't Miss Liza at the gate – only a young woman she had never laid eyes on before.

'Hello?'

Mrs G sighed. She was in no mood for this kind of thing. It was a regular occurrence, this; all manner of people would walk up through Beverly Hills every morning and knock on each gate in turn to ask for money, or food, or work. There was one set who claimed their house had miraculously been burnt out every week and were always looking for whatever you could spare. Mrs G didn't mind the concocted stories; she usually had a soft spot for such people, and as long as

Timothy was out of the way, she would give them whatever she could. However, it was an angry and distracted Mrs G who finally opened the front door that Wednesday morning.

'Good morning,' Mrs G called out, an unusual sharpness to her voice.

The young woman at the other side of the gate just stood there, her mouth opening and closing but without making another sound, as if she were suddenly ashamed and unable to bring herself to ask for whatever handout she had come for.

'Can I help you?' Mrs G snapped.

The young woman was silent and then shook her head. She mouthed the words, *Sorry, miss,* and began to turn away from the gate.

Mrs G was about to close her front door, but then something in her melted. She was suddenly disappointed in herself. On this particular morning, when she had every reason to suspend her faith in the world and in people and in honesty, she decided to reaffirm that faith. She opened the door again. 'My dear,' she called out to the young woman who was now walking away, 'by any chance are you looking for work?'

The young woman turned back. She seemed genuinely surprised and almost on the verge of laughter. She spoke for the first time. 'Yes, ma'am. I'm looking for work.'

'Well, come in then,' said Mrs G. The principal forced herself to ignore a nagging voice inside her, *So you're really going to let yet another little thief inside your home? You haven't learnt your lesson yet? And what will Timothy say? This one doesn't even come with a recommendation! You don't know her from Adam! Ha! She might just go off with everything!*

170

Mrs G went to open the gate. 'Come in, my dear. It just so happens that I am looking for someone to help with the housework. Is that the kind of thing you can do?'

'Yes, ma'am,' the young woman nodded.

'All right then. Follow me.' Mrs G led the stranger into her home and then from room to room – the master bedroom, the two guest bedrooms and another bedroom, which she explained would not really require much cleaning. 'This is my son's room, but he's been away for a while now.' She smiled. 'He's about to start his PhD at Harvard University. My goodness, they grow up so fast. Do you have children?'

The young woman did not answer. She had fallen back into her strange silence.

'Well, anyway. If you take the job, which would start next Monday, then every couple of weeks or so you can just open the windows to air it out a little.'

Mrs G then showed the stranger the washing machine and explained how to operate it; she showed her the utility room where the ironing board and the cleaning products were kept, realising then that all of her detergents and bottles of bleach and starch had been stolen as well. She sighed, making a mental note to replace them. 'So that is what the work would entail. Do you have any questions for me?'

'What happened to Blanche?'

Mrs G's eyes widened. She was genuinely surprised. 'You knew Blanche?'

'Not very well, ma'am. But I know she used to work here.'

'Blanche has migrated. Gone to take care of her sister in the States.'

The young woman nodded. They were now in the living room, and Mrs G observed her guest as she walked the length of a display cabinet, running her index finger across its smooth guango surface before picking up a green and turquoise vase. Mrs G flinched. It was an expensive vase. 'It's a Cecil Cooper,' she offered, and then felt silly for thinking the young woman would know or care.

But the stranger only smiled. 'No,' she said, almost absently. 'This is Norma Harrack.' She put down the vase and took up the one that was right beside it. 'This one is the Cecil Cooper.'

Mrs G almost choked. For the first time she looked on the young woman properly and with a sort of wonder. The soon-to-be helper's focus had already moved on. Her eyes were darting around the room as if to take in the whole house. She spotted a bookshelf in the corner and walked over to it. Once again she ran an index finger across its length and seemed to linger a little on each title.

Mrs G cleared her throat. 'I don't even know your name, by the way.'

'Sorry, Miss G, ma'am. You can call me Miss G.'

Mrs G chuckled. 'That will be confusing. People call me Mrs G. It's Mrs Claudia Garrick, really.'

Miss G turned back to the principal and observed her as carefully as she had been observing the art and the books on the shelves. Mrs G felt strange, as if she was the one now being assessed. She stood up straighter.

'What's so confusing bout that, ma'am? You are Mrs and I am Miss. I think people will be able to tell the difference.' Miss G paused. 'You're a teacher, yes?'

It was hardly a question, and Mrs G understood that she was definitely the one being interviewed now. Where had the timidity she had witnessed at the gate gone, she wondered?

She certainly had not got the full measure of this young woman, and it made her both uncomfortable and curious. She nodded her head. 'Yes, my dear. I am a teacher. Well, I used to be.'

'That's good enough,' Miss G said, as if satisfied. 'I will help you clean the house then. But I will want you to help me with something. If you can.'

'And what is that?'

Miss G turned once again to the bookcase. 'Some subjects, ma'am. I don't have any, and I would like to study for them. You can help me with that?'

'You mean, like O Level subjects?'

'Yes, ma'am.'

Mrs G felt something warm spreading inside her, a sense of possibility and opportunity, not just for the young woman who stood in front of her but also for herself. She could actually teach again. She could do something that really mattered. She believed she now understood something of the effect Miss G had on her – the slightly fragile pride with which the young woman carried herself – and Mrs G decided that she admired her attitude. She was not a religious woman, Mrs G – a lapsed Anglican – but the thought came to her those three years ago that maybe the other five helpers had not worked out because they had not been destined to work out. Maybe all this time she had been waiting for this particular young woman, Miss G, to arrive at her door.

Mrs G answered, 'Yes, my dear. I think I can definitely help you with some subjects.'

19

But what was it really that had taken Miss G up through Beverly Hills that morning, to shout *Hello* and knock on the gate of the Garricks' house? Despite what she said, she had not been looking for a job. She had one of those already – a modest job working the till at a cafeteria near Matilda's Corner at the foot of Beverly Hills. And neither had she been looking for anyone to help her with her O Level subjects. That was something that came to her on the spot. And although she welcomed the help, she was more than capable of doing it all on her own.

The truth is, for Miss G, every step up that hill had been a step not towards a future, but towards a past. And when Mrs Garrick had opened the door and said, 'Good morning', what Miss G had experienced was a small panic of the heart; a widening of the eyes; an O of the mouth.

So I am here again, she thought. *Back in Beverly Hills – back at the Garricks' house.* But she could not explain this to Mrs G. Though she had walked up the hill with such determination, when she saw Mrs G her mouth had gone completely dry. She could not find the words to say why she was there that morning, and how it was that she had been there before. She did not know how to provide Mrs Garrick with a context.

Instead, it was Mrs G who offered one to her.

'Are you looking for work?' Mrs Garrick had asked, and Miss G had almost laughed. *This poor whitewoman,* she thought. *She can think of no other context in which a young woman such as me should end up at a house such as this.* But it was easier, wasn't it? It was so much easier and less awkward than the truth. It gave Miss G a quicker way to get inside the house, and so she accepted this false context. She said to herself that as soon as she was inside, she would tell Mrs G everything, the long speech she had practised, but it didn't happen that morning. She began working at the house the following Monday, and said to herself, one day, one day very soon, I will sit Mrs G down and give her a cup of mint tea to calm her nerves and then I will explain everything. I going to say to Mrs G, 'Ma'am, I am an honest woman and I am not here to hustle you for no money. That is not what this is about. But we are connected in another way, ma'am. There is another context in which we ought to know and speak to each other.' But days became weeks, and weeks became months, and, just like that, the months became three years.

Instead of explaining herself or her past, Miss G threw herself into her new work – both the housework and the schoolwork – cooking and cleaning and washing during the day, then reading and studying and revising in the afternoons. Every evening that house in Beverly Hills transformed itself into a virtual classroom.

Mrs G threw herself completely into it as well. She raided her son's bedroom for whatever O Level syllabuses and textbooks he had left behind. She went to Sangster's Bookstore to buy the shortfall. She also bought exercise books, pens, pencils, a ream of graph paper, a calculator and a geometry set. She went to bed late at night teaching herself things before trying to teach them to Miss G.

At first, her aim was simple – she was going to help Miss G get through one or two subjects. But of course, she did not know anything about Miss G's past, and had greatly underestimated her helper's abilities. Things dawned on the employer slowly. More than once it had seemed to her that Miss G wasn't learning anything for the first time; instead, she was remembering things she had once known. Miss G picked up on things too quickly – almost effortlessly – like someone relearning the use of a muscle. After only five months, the helper took three subjects: mathematics, English language and English literature. She got grade A in all of them. Mrs G saw the paper bearing these results and her mouth opened and closed several times, soundlessly, like a fish.

Mrs G rolled up her sleeves and decided to make things harder the next round. 'All right. I see that you can handle this, Miss G. So let us do five more subjects,' and together they embarked on advanced mathematics, geography, history, chemistry and biology. Mrs G herself never quite got the hang of the advanced mathematics or the chemistry, but it did not matter. Miss G did, and once again she sat the five exams and got grade A for everything. Mrs G was astonished. This was the brightest pupil she had ever taught. It seemed to her that Miss G was the kind of person for whom the cliché was true: she had a fertile mind, which is to say that once a bit of knowledge was planted in her brain, it grew on its own and produced more knowledge. Eventually it became its own thick forest, but one that Miss G could always navigate her way through. She ruminated on things and they became more complex in her mind; they produced a pleasing density. She did not separate one subject from another, allowing her knowledge of mathematics to graft itself onto her knowledge of biology, or her knowledge of history to cross-pollinate her knowledge of chemistry, and so on. She was a natural academic. She saw connections in things where most people would not.

By now Miss G was taking down book after book from Mrs G's shelves, going through them rapidly. Some evenings Mrs G would come home from Augustown Primary to find all the housework done, and Miss G in her son's bedroom, there on the bed, reading three books at once. Caught in this manner, Miss G would jump off the bed. 'Sorry, Mrs G. I never mean anything by it. I was just resting my foot and reading.'

'No, no . . . there's nothing to apologise for,' Mrs G would say dismissively, but she always felt a little queer.

'OK. We will do A Levels now,' the principal said one day, desperate to find something, anything, that would challenge Miss G.

Timothy Garrick, who came in late each evening, often found the two women at the dining table still working. He tried in his own way to intervene, to talk some sense into his wife. One night in the dark, as they were patting their pillows and taking their usual shapes in the bed, he said to her, 'Claudia, what is really going on with you and that helper, though? Don't you think you are taking this too far now? She is not your daughter, for godsake.'

Mr Garrick regretted saying this as soon as it was out of his mouth. He knew his wife would think, as he was now thinking, about the child they had lost over fifteen years ago, the daughter they never had, the little sister they could not give to their son. The wound of it was suddenly raw.

Mrs G jumped out of the bed with an agility that fright-ened her husband. She stormed over to the light switch and violently flicked it on. The brightness from the ceiling bulbs and the anger in Mrs G's eyes glared down on what had be-come a trembling man.

'Now you look here, Timothy,' Mrs G said to him. 'I do not interfere with your work, and you will not interfere with mine. That girl is doing just fine. Just fine! And I want to tell you something else. When she gets into university, which mark my words she will, we are going to help her with her school fees, and I don't want to hear a peep from you about it. She has the brains and we have the finances, and that is that. You understand me?'

'All right, all right,' Mr Garrick said plaintively. 'I was just making a simple . . .' but Timothy Garrick looked at his wife again and thought better of it. 'Yes, Claudia. I'm sorry. I never mean anything by it.'

Mrs G made a sound in her throat and then turned off the lights a second time. She climbed back into bed but there remained, for that night, a frostiness between the two.

Mrs G remembers that night now as she sits with Miss G on a bench in the garden. They are under the shade of a sweet almond tree. Neither of them is looking at the other. Rather, their gaze travels down the hill towards Mona and further across towards Augustown. If they are avoiding each other's eyes, they are avoiding even more than that: they are avoid-ing the unopened envelope which Miss G holds in her hand. Though it was delivered to the Garricks' post office box, it is addressed to her – Ms Gina Elizabeth McDonald. In the top right corner is a blue pelican – the crest of the University of the West Indies.

Mrs G knows that there is something unbridgeable between herself and the helper – something to do with class and colour. Over the past year, there have been times when she has turned around to find Miss G looking at her with something in her eyes which, if she had to name it, she would call 'disapproval' – though it wasn't quite that. In any case, on such occasions Miss G would look away quickly, or busy herself suddenly, as if knowing she had been found out, and a queer feeling would come over the principal. Mrs G understands that of the two of them, it is Miss G who has the better mind, and so she feels strangely judged by the young woman's silent looks.

To no one's surprise, Miss G has received all As in her A Levels, and so it is almost certain that she has got into the Faculty of Law. The envelope she now holds in her hand is pleasingly fat. Rejection, Mrs G knows, comes in thin envelopes, if it comes at all: single sheets of paper with white space like snow around a cold and callous message. 'We regret to inform you that your application was not successful.' Barely ever more than that. But good news comes in envelopes such as this – thick envelopes – the news explained over multiple sheets of paper. So Mrs G isn't sure why Miss G is just sitting here, refusing to break the seal. In fact, Mrs G has never seen her helper so emotional or so vulnerable. Miss G looks down on the letter again and her eyes well up.

Mrs G tries again. 'Why don't you just open it, Miss G? Get it over with.'

Miss G wipes her face on her blouse and then looks down the hill towards Augustown. 'Ma'am,' she begins slowly, 'I can't thank you enough for all the help you give me so far. I never expect people like you to help people like me.' Miss G is now looking Mrs G straight in the eye. 'You are a good woman, Mrs G. Better than I did expect.'

Claudia Garrick smiles, feeling at once moved, but also that there is a history behind this remark that she might never know.

'I sorry, ma'am,' Miss G continues, 'but I can't open the letter here. I do all these things – get my subjects, apply to university – without the two most important people in my life knowing: Ma Taffy, who raise me, and my little boy, Kaia. So I think I owe them this part of it. I need to open the letter in front of them.'

Mrs G turns away quickly, hoping Miss G will not see the sudden flash of hurt in her eyes. It is the hurt of a mother. The two women sit in silence, the unopened letter creating a large space between them.

A breeze blows and ruffles the leaves of the almond tree, and on that breeze comes the snippet of a song.

Fly away home to Zion, Fly . . .

The song dies with the wind.

'What was that?' Mrs G asks, her heart beating fast. It is the most beautiful voice she has ever heard.

Miss G raises her shoulders in a shrug, but she too has felt strangely moved. A rash of goose pimples covers her arms and the hairs stand up on the back of her neck.

Another gust blows and with it comes a second snatch of song.

Fly away home to Zion, Fly away home . . .

The two women stand up now. They strain their eyes down the hill, trying without binoculars to see Augustown.

It is the dreadful day of the autoclaps, and these are the four things Mrs G will always remember about it:

1) The little boy whose eyes had been swollen and red from crying. She had passed him at the gate of the school. She was leaving work early, excited to deliver the letter she had picked up to Miss G. It was only later that she would realise she should have stopped to speak to the boy. She didn't know then that he was connected to everything.

2) The small bit of song that rode on the wind all the way from Augustown, past Mona and up to the sweet almond tree under which she and Miss G had been sitting.

3) The unopened letter that sat between her and Miss G.

4) And Miss G herself: Gina Elizabeth McDonald, 8 January 1961–11 April 1982. There will be no burial and there will be no tombstone, but this much is certain: hers will be the second death on the day of the autoclaps.

20

When Kaia left the classroom, the thing that hit him hardest was the coolness of the day pressing down directly on his head. To everyone else the day was terribly humid, but without his dreadlocks it had felt like a kind of December day, like a Christmas breeze was blowing on his head. His head felt strange to him, and, with it, his whole body. He could no longer find his balance, and so he wobbled out of the classroom rather than walked.

Out there in the corridor he began to cry, but in all, he cried for less than ten minutes. What should have been a torrential cloudburst – what should have been the kind of drowning rain that washes the loose marl off the roads and then deposits it as a ruining layer of white in all the nearby yards, the kind of rain that gets beneath the mango trees and then leans them into zinc houses – passed too quickly. Whenever he cried, his grandmother would always tell him, *You need a backbone, boy.* She thought this was the way to raise a man-child without quite understanding that sometimes it takes backbone to cry the long length of tears required.

One day Ma Taffy will stop to consider this – that maybe if Kaia had kept wailing, maybe if he had kept within him that indignation and that fighting spirit, maybe if he had found a deeper well of tears to draw from, it would have taken him all the way into the principal's office: Mrs G, who would have listened to him and who would have marched to classroom 2B and told Mr Saint-Josephs in no uncertain terms that he should never return to the school; Mrs G, who would have known then that the right thing to do was to put Kaia into the front seat of her car and drive him to his home; the principal, who would have drawn the eyes of all Augustown on to her for driving her big car into the tiny zinc-fenced lane. She would have parked the car right there, got out and walked up to the verandah where she, Ma Taffy, would be sitting, and Mrs G would have explained clearly and briefly to the old woman what had happened that day; Mrs G, who would have known instinctively to do this without any grovelling or any wringing round of her hands, because her presence alone would have signalled the desperation of her apology. And though Ma Taffy knew this, she would have raised her voice at the principal – would have called down brimstone and thunder and judgement – but it would only have been because she too was playing the role expected of her; because the ears of Augustown would have been listening, and would have needed to hear her make the most of this one opportunity when one of their own could give a piece of their mind to a *big smaddy* in society. But Ma Taffy would have understood the principal's integrity; the old woman would have heard it from the very beginning, from the stuttered sound of her car engine approaching the house – and Ma Taffy would have respected this big woman of society for having willingly made herself small in the presence of a small woman like herself. Ma Taffy would have accepted the apology, and would have known how to explain things to Gina, and they would have accepted that although a great wrong had been done to their family, this was one of the few times that Babylon had acknowledged such wrongdoing and had offered them an I.O.U., something for future payment.

But none of it happened like that. When Kaia stepped out of classroom 2B, he had flung his head back in the doorway and the first wailing sound came out of him. It was a long *waaaaaaaah*, a sound like a siren. He then took a sharp, hiccupy breath and let out another sound much like the first. His tears made the world blurry. He dragged his skinny feet down the corridor past other classrooms. Boys in their khaki uniforms and girls in their blue plaid cotton dresses turned to observe him for a second, but just as quickly they turned back to their lessons.

A teacher had stepped out from her classroom into Kaia's path. The little boy stopped. The teacher seemed like a peach-clad giant in front of him; her matronly linen suit was starch stiff and her stout arms were akimbo. Kaia hiccuped and wailed again. He held his arms out, thinking that she might lift him up. The woman sucked her teeth. 'Lickle bwoy, you just hush up de damn cowbawling and go to where you going!' She made a funny face, as if she was about to spit. 'Disgraceful!' She looked the boy up and down and then flounced back into her classroom.

Kaia had continued in the general direction of Mrs G's office, but already his crying had diminished in volume and conviction. He had begun to doubt himself. He wondered suddenly if Mr Saint-Josephs might even have been right to do what he had done. Adults were always right. They had their reasons. Maybe what had happened really was because he was just too rude. He wasn't sure. He had never felt particularly rude, even on those nights when he found it hard to fall asleep, no matter how tightly he closed his eyes, or those mornings when he refused to eat all the callaloo on his plate and his mother or Ma Taffy would tell him off; and even then they would be holding his hand softly, or stroking his head, something to make him know he wasn't really being rude at all.

But what if the principal also told him to stop the damn cowbawling? *Just stop it!* What if she too made a funny face and told him he was disgraceful? He turned and walked towards the school gate. He had stopped crying completely.

As he approached the gate, the security guard opened it wide. Kaia thought this was for him, as he hadn't heard the vehicle behind him. It was Mrs G. She began to drive out of the gate, but turned and looked Kaia in the eye. She stopped the car and rolled down her window.

'Are you all right, son?'

He looked at her but could not find any words.

Mrs G frowned. After a moment, she wound the window back up and drove away.

Kaia walked through the open gate of the school and back onto the dry roads of Augustown. He continued hiccuping, but the *waaaaaah*ing siren had ceased. Already he was falling into the silence he would never escape from, which is not to say that he became mute. Rather, he was folding himself into himself. He was learning how to become withdrawn and surly. He was learning how to be defeated. And once learnt, it was a lesson Kaia would find impossible to unlearn.

He reached around to touch his dreadlocks, but his hands only found empty air. Tears flooded his eyes again and

185

he cried silently. His mother had always told him that his strength was in his dreadlocks. She had told him that his dreadlocks were his lion's mane. Whenever something bad happened to him, Ma Taffy would sit in a corner muttering something about a backbone, but his mother would hold him close and then cup his chin with her hand and lift up his face so that he was looking at her. 'You see this right here?' she would say, reaching round to touch his locks. 'You is a lion. Just like Ma Taffy. Just like me. We is lions, Kaia. Conquering lions. I not saying you mustn't be up-set, and I not saying you mustn't cry either. But whenever something bad happen, you just touch your natty locks and remind youself that you is a lion. We stronger than all the bullshit that happen around us. You understand me?'

But what could Kaia hold onto now? Maybe he was no longer a lion like his mummy or his grandma.

Less than ten minutes. It was not enough tears for what had happened to him.

Still, Ma Taffy, over a mile away, had heard him. And also, she had smelt the strange, choking sweetness of the day.

21

Ma Taffy is not one for favourites, but if you press her she might admit the difficult truth that of the three nieces she has raised, Gina is the one she loves the most. But this truth is not an easy one to face, because if she does, then Ma Taffy will have to own up to an even harder truth: that of the three girls, Gina has been the greatest disappointment.

Ma Taffy had not expected great things of the other two. This was no slight on them. It was just Ma Taffy's pragmatic understanding of the world. She was a poor woman raising poor children in a poor place. What more hope could she have for them but that they survive? Every morning she hoped that they would be so blessed as to avoid bullets and knives and the various schemes of Babylon. She also hoped that when they were older, they would not be too acquaint-ed with hunger, and that, in whatever way, they might also know a portion of love. That was enough to hope for. That was plenty. And if, on top of surviving, the girls managed to finish high school, or go to community college, or university even, it would have just been brawta – an extra measure giv-en unto them. If such things happened, then praise Jah, but if such brawta did not happen, then so what? She couldn't really complain because she hadn't even hoped for it. Ma

Taffy's first two girls did survive. They had grown up to be honest women with heads firmly attached to their bodies, and that was enough for Ma Taffy.

But with Gina, things had always been different. This was the child with brains – the kind of brains you could use to do great things. It was Gina who had helped Ma Taffy through the early months of her blindness, and without even knowing what she was doing. Ma Taffy owed the child a debt.

In the aftermath of the collapse of Ma Taffy's roof, the people of Augustown had been helpful. The men who worked in construction had pinched a half-bag of cement here and a half-bag of cement there, along with sheets of zinc, and they had put the roof back up in record time. Ma Taffy mumbled thanks to whoever was in earshot, trying to be grateful, but then went straight back into that room and stayed there for weeks. She was bitter. People came to visit her, but she would not say much. People arrived with food, but she hardly ate. Blindness to Ma Taffy felt like the beginnings of death, and so she was waiting for the whole thing to consume her.

It was Gina who changed things. Whenever the little girl sat there at the side of the bed, silent, observing her aunt, Ma Taffy would feel a flutter of sensation travelling up her spine and around her face. She realised that what she was feeling was the child's mind at work, and it astonished her. So one day she tried an experiment. She formed in her mind the thought: *Gina, go and get me a cup of tea.*

'What kind of tea you want, Auntie?' Gina asked.

'Cerasee,' Ma Taffy answered aloud.

Gina rose from her seat and went into the kitchen to prepare the tea.

'Well, look at that!' Ma Taffy whispered.

Without knowing it, Gina had taught her aunt how to be silent and how to reach into the minds of others. Ma Taffy now knew how to discern Gina's presence, and so she taught herself how to discern the presence of others. Soon she would teach herself how to discern smells and sounds, even from a distance. She was becoming a woman who could hear and taste and smell what other people could not. It was therefore not the simple fact of blindness that made her so alert, so perceptive – it was her relationship with Gina.

So Ma Taffy began to hope, not just that her youngest niece would survive, but that she would thrive as well. She hoped that this little girl would be the one to know and understand Babylon from the inside out, and that one day she would be able to rise over it all.

'But why spend time with these lessons, Auntie?' Gina would complain some evenings, bored with school and trying to use Ma Taffy's own logic against her. 'All of this is just whiteman knowledge.'

'True,' Ma Taffy would agree. 'That is true. But if you learn whiteman knowledge even better than the whiteman, then one day you will know how to use the tools of Babylon against Babylon.'

Ma Taffy began to whisper things to Gina – things she had never told the other two girls, things that only uptown people ever said to their children. *You can be anything you want to be, girl*, Ma Taffy said, *so long as you put your mind to it. You can accomplish it.* With all her heart Ma Taffy believed this. She even hoped for it. But then one day Gina upped and got pregnant, and for the whole nine months of the pregnancy, Ma Taffy did not know.

189

On the night when Kaia was to be born, Gina woke up from a nightmare. At first she thought it was her own screaming that had pulled her out of sleep, but when she opened her eyes it seemed to be one of those perfectly still nights in Augustown. The sweet smell of crushed bougainvillea wafted up from between her legs. She also felt a spreading wetness, and then a more urgent feeling: her stomach seemed to be pulling into itself violently, but in the next moment, it felt as if it was exploding. She screamed this time, realising it was this strange violence happening inside her own body, and not the nightmare, that had caused her to wake up.

Ma Taffy was standing in the doorway. 'Gina, what happen?' Gina could hardly see the old woman.

'Don't turn on the lights, Auntie. Just leave them off.' She said through gritted teeth.

'I ask you what happen, Gina?'

'Nothing, Auntie. Go to your bed. And leave the lights off.'

'What I turning on no goddamn lights for?!'

Gina's scream cut off the old woman as another contraction tore through the fifteen-year-old's body.

'To raasclawt!' Ma Taffy gasped.

'Is a baby, Auntie. And it coming now.'

'Stay calm, child. Uhm. I going to get some . . . some water. Yes. And towels. Just . . . just stay calm.' The old woman began to shuffle out to get the items, but Gina could hear her walking into things – the table, the wall, the chair. Ma Taffy walking into things? How strange! And it was in this way that the girl knew she was still asleep; that she had only woken from one dream into another.

She opened her eyes a second time, this time finally waking up. She knew that the labour pains were real, though. Another contraction came and she stuffed a pillow into her mouth while yanking off her panties. She was determined not to make a sound. She was going to do this by herself.

She got up out of the bed and walked over to the window. She held on to the burglar bars and stooped. She let the pain of the contractions help her to push. She heard something plop onto the ground, and the green-brown smell of her faeces reached up to her nostrils, and it was the shame of this much more than the pain that made tears wash her face.

She cried silently as she pushed. It felt as if this baby was going to tear her in two. She felt the lips of her lower parts opening wide as if they too wanted to scream. She squeezed the burglar bars even more tightly till it seemed they were cutting into her hands. Her small knees were trembling. You could not distinguish her tears from the sweat that now washed her entire body. She took quick and shallow breaths, and tried to remember everything she had read beforehand about this moment. She knew the baby would come first, and then the placenta, and then she would have to use string and tie the umbilical cord four inches away from the child. Gina gritted her teeth and pushed the baby all the way out. She crumpled to the floor like a disused rag, lying there in the mess of water, blood and faeces, and in the umbilical tangle of her just-born baby.

In her own bedroom Ma Taffy had just woken up. The smell of crushed bougainvillea was in her nostrils. *That is a smell like a woman's water breaking.* She thought this without effort, almost in a dream state, and then turned on her pillow to go back to sleep. She began to drift off again but was dimly aware of Gina's feet moving about the small house. She jolted up. Now fully awake, her mind began replaying things she had not noticed in the past few months – things she had found strange but had dismissed without trying to make too much sense of them. She sniffed the air and smelt the bougainvillea again. She listened to the soft footsteps of Gina. She thought about the past few months and a sudden knowing lodged itself under Ma Taffy's ribcage.

She got out of her bed and ambled quickly towards the bathroom. She was muttering the whole way. 'Wicked bloodclawt whore of Babylon! Dutty Jezebel gyal! Whore!'

She got to the bathroom where Gina was now kneeling in front of the toilet. Ma Taffy's voice came out, thin and sharp as a whip. 'Is a good thing mi can't even see you. Cause you is a dirty and wicked whore. You is a lickle agent of Babylon. Fire pon you, child.'

The girl began to tremble as she held the tiny baby over the toilet bowl like an offering.

Ma Taffy continued. 'Is coulda never you mi did raise. Raise you from you so small. No sah. It coulda never. I don't know you at all no more, Gina. What could really make you think of doing such a thing? Eeeh? To kill off yu own little baby? That is murder! That is wickedness.'

A sound of snot and tears came from the girl's mouth. 'How you know, Auntie?'

Ma Taffy was breathing heavily. 'Just cause mi old and blind don't mean you should take mi for a fool. All these months mi never understand what did happen to you – why you stop go school, and the way . . . the way you just close off from me.' Ma Taffy paused. An unexpected bubble of emotion had risen up into her throat. 'You never do that before, you know. You never close yourself off from me. Not like that. I did think maybe you just reach a age where you was really becoming your own woman, and I say to myself, maybe you just need the space to become what you was becoming. That's what I say. I say, maybe you need that space.' Ma Taffy eased herself down to the linoleum floor and her yellow eye gleamed in the sliver of white light that came into the house from the street lamp outside. Her eye was wet.

'Sometimes I think I know you better than the other two. I don't see you, but is like I learn how to . . . eem . . . what is the word?'

'Perceive?' Gina offered, as she often did, still helping to complete her aunt's sentences.

'Yes. That is the word. I learn how fi perceive you. But I realise I can't do it no more. I come into a room and I almost walk right into you cause I don't know you is even there. But is you, Gina. Is you was the one shutting yourself off from me. Like you decide to close a door between me and you. Like you decide to be invisible. But is a evil silence you holding between us, girl. And this thing, this thing you thinking of doing, that is even more evilous.'

Ma Taffy stayed there for a while. No more words passed between the two. They perceived each other in the dark, Gina opening the door she had closed. 'I'm sorry,' she said to Ma Taffy from within herself. 'Thank you,' Ma Taffy said from within herself.

The old woman stood up at last and returned to her bedroom. She never went back to sleep, though. Instead, she

193

listened to the sound of the baby that had now started crying; the sound of Gina's feet as she walked out from the
bathroom; the sound of Gina's voice as she cooed the baby
to sleep.

22

The day broke, and Ma Taffy lifted the as-yet-to-be-named boy-child and surveyed him as carefully as a cartographer might survey a new piece of land. She ran her fingers over his tiny toes, his fat legs, his little penis. She felt his arms and pulled each of his ten fingers. She did her examination with great care, learning the shape of the boy and making sure everything was as it should be.

Then her fingers found his face. The baby opened his mouth and gurgled. It was a pleasing sound.

Ma Taffy smiled as she felt his lips, his eyes, his nose, the shape of his forehead and his cheekbones. She stopped short. She ran her fingers over his face again. And then again. She didn't know why this new revelation surprised her even more than the fact that Gina had been pregnant all along.

Gina was observing this examination. At first she turned her own face to the window as if ashamed, but then she turned back and pulled the boy out of the old woman's arms.

'I going to call him Kaia,' Gina said. The words came out with more obstinacy than she had intended, but she was answering a question Ma Taffy had not yet thought to ask, or rather she was refusing her permission to ask it. For it was true what Ma Taffy had said the night before; the girl was becoming a woman and needed a space for her own secrets. She had reopened the door between herself and her aunt, but only partially.

'Kaia?' Ma Taffy asked.

'Yes. Kaia,' Gina said with finality.

Ma Taffy bit her lips.

Kaia. Zulu for home, though Ma Taffy did not know this. Instead, she knew of Kaya as weed – ganja – or else, Kaya as hair. Thick, nappy, African hair, a kind of hair that this boy certainly would not have. It was a strong, African-sounding name. A Rasta name. Ma Taffy began to think about names, and the fact that she had changed her own from Irene to Irie. She had given herself her own Rasta name. She disliked that so many of her people walked around with names like Lisa or Robert or George – names that tried to diminish the greatest part of who they were, of their history; names that weren't even names, but erasures. And maybe this was her hesitation with this name, Kaia – that it, too, seemed to be an erasure. It was trying to rub out part of the child. And did it matter, Ma Taffy wondered, that the part of him that was being erased by his name was the part that could make life easier for the boy? Or maybe she felt that a Rasta name was the kind of name a man or woman had to find on their own. You couldn't just be born with it. You had to grow into it. It could not be passed down so simply from parent to child. Ma Taffy felt a complicated thing inside her, but she did not have the words to unravel or make sense of that thing, and on this occasion she did not know how to ask Gina for the words she was seeking.

If they had been able to talk about it – if Gina hadn't

closed the door on these questions – she would have explained to Ma Taffy that it wasn't the child's half whiteness she was trying to diminish. Not exactly. Rather, it was a specific man – a boy, really – that she was trying to forget.

One of Ma Taffy's most constant bits of advice to her girls was this: *Make a fool kiss you, that is one thing, but to make a kiss fool you! That is even worser. Don't make no man turn you into no fool!* Sometimes she replaced the word 'kiss' with something even cruder.

Gina had taken this advice seriously, and was cautious around boys. She wasn't prudish, for this was not Ma Taffy's intention. She kissed boys when she felt like it, and twice she had made a boy touch her in her private place. But there was a line that had to do with her own mind and her own comfort, and no one was able to push past that. As well, Gina believed Ma Taffy's words – that she could be anything she wanted to be – and she was determined to be someone who would rise up out of Augustown. The boys from the community were therefore unattractive to her. Sometimes they accused her: 'You think you better than we! Don't it? Bright gyal from the ghetto.' And Gina would nod. 'I don't think I better than you. I know it.'

The Augustown boys had no chance and they gave up trying, but the grown men were more determined. There was something about a schoolgirl in her uniform that made them act all silly. Gina had ripened to a perfect age, and each man felt he wanted to be the one to pick her. When she walked to school they would whistle and *pssst* and offer her all manner of things: clothes, money, trips. On school mornings, Gina was therefore never surprised when a car would slow down behind her and then pull up alongside her, a big man with his face outside the window, his tongue outside his mouth, sometimes grabbing for her. She was used to all this. So when she heard the car slow down behind her on that fateful morning and then pull up alongside, she took a deep breath and, without even turning her head, she shouted, 'Why you don't go home and fuck yu blasted wife and stop bother school pickney?! Yu raas pervert, yu!'

She spun around then, ready to see the man's stunned face and take whatever abuse he was going to mete out. She was taken aback, then, to see a boy, hardly older than she was, behind the wheel of a blue Honda. And he was smiling at her. She was not prepared for such a thing. This white boy was smiling at her.

'I don't have wife or pickney,' he said, half laughing, 'but you look like you're rushing. You want a lift?'

She stammered. It was embarrassment more than anything else that made her get into the car.

The boy examined her uniform, the maroon crest on the breast of a khaki tunic. 'I guess you're going to Mona High?' he asked. It was a long walk in the sun but barely a three-minute drive.

Gina nodded uselessly. She knew how to resist the boys of Augustown, and also the men, but this boy seemed to come from a world far, far away.

They said little on that first, short car ride, but the next morning his car pulled up behind her again. And the morning after that. And after a short time Gina would just wait for him at a regular spot – under a poui tree, its yellow blossoms falling into her hair.

His name was Matthew, and over the next week she

198

learnt that he had just finished high school – Campion College – and was taking a year out before going off to university abroad. He was helping his parents for the year, doing
odd jobs for them, so every morning he dropped his mother
at work in Augustown and then borrowed her car for the
day to do the errands he had been assigned.

They talked about little things – Matthew, about his errands; Gina, about the classes she had to take. Sometimes
Matthew quizzed Gina on the subjects she was studying. He
did not mean to be patronising, but realised he had been
whenever he was taken aback by the fluency of her answers.
Sometimes Gina explained concepts to him that he had never
fully understood himself, and he began to look at her
differently.

'You know,' he said one morning, 'you're just as bright as
any of the kids at Campion.'

'And why that should surprise you?' she snapped, for she
understood more than he did. This boy could only make
sense of her if he compared her to the people from his
world. But she was not from his world, and she did not want
him to forget that. 'You feel that is only uptown people that
supposed to be smart?'

'It's not that,' Matthew insisted. 'I was just wondering how
you ended up at Mona High. Come on, Gina . . . be honest.
It's not a good school. You could have gone anywhere.'

'Well, maybe I don't have Campion money.'

'It's not about money,' he shot back. To some extent he
was right. In the island's Grade Six Common Entrance exams,
students could pick whichever high school they wanted to
go to. School fees were the same across the island, so as long
as a child got the grades, they could get into the school of

their choice. Few people would have put down Mona High as their first choice. It was the kind of school that accepted the remainder of students, those who didn't get the grades to attend the schools they had actually picked.

'I didn't think too much about what school I wanted to go to,' Gina confessed. 'My two cousins, they're like my sisters. They went to Mona High, so that's where I chose.'

'Well, that's a pity.'

'Excuse me?!'

'I'm sorry, but it is.'

'And why exactly is that? Because I don't go to no snobbish uptown school?'

'No. Because . . . I don't know.' Matthew paused. He knew he was putting his foot right back into his mouth, but he shrugged and risked it. 'Maybe you could have achieved more if you had gone to another school.'

'Achieved more?' she was still incredulous.

'No. Not that. But had more opportunities.'

'But Matthew, if I get the same grades at Mona as you did get at Campion, then what difference it make?'

'Yes, I suppose,' Matthew conceded and said no more. But even then, a big and uncomfortable truth started to sit between them. This was Jamaica, after all. He knew it and she knew it. Where you were born mattered. Where you lived mattered even more. And if you were born in the wrong place and also lived in the wrong place, then where you went to school mattered as much as water matters to a thirsty man in the desert. It made a difference.

But they ignored this thing that was sitting between them, this incredible distance between their two worlds. It made no sense in the small confines of that blue Honda. It made

200

no sense in relation to how close they were beginning to feel towards each other, and how much closer they wanted to get. The daily drive from the poui trees to Mona High School went on for weeks, and something like love began to grow in that car.

23

'I don't even feel like go to school today,' Gina complained one morning. 'Just the same old boring classes. I think I even know more than the teachers now.'

She had been practising this complaint for days. She was trying to create a situation that they both wanted.

Matthew turned to her, his eyes momentarily off the road, his Adam's apple moving up and down his neck. He turned back, his hands holding the steering wheel tighter than usual. 'Do you want to see where I live, then? It's not far – just up there in Beverly Hills. Blanche will be there, the housekeeper. But she's cool. It will be all right.'

Gina nodded.

The blue Honda went past Mona High and continued down Mona Road. It was the first time Gina had taken the turn off that went up into the affluent neighbourhood, the first time she would find herself at the Garricks' house – not knowing then that she would return years later.

'I want to show you something first,' Matthew said as they got out of the car. He took her round to the back of the house and they looked at the city spread out below them. He intertwined his fingers with hers. 'Beautiful, isn't it?'

Gina had never seen Kingston from above like this, and

suddenly she wasn't sure that she liked heights. It was making her nauseous. She closed her eyes in order to steady herself.

Matthew took her silence as a sort of childishness. 'Lord, man, Gina. You just like to be contrary. Just appreciate the view for what it is.'

Gina opened her eyes again and took a breath. She wrestled her hand out of his and pointed towards Papine. 'Ma Taffy's house is somewhere down there?'

Matthew took her hand again and rotated her whole body about thirty degrees.

'No . . . it would be somewhere there. Down there is Augustown. You just have to look for the white crater in the hillside. Do you see? Amazing, don't you think?'

'So people like me live our whole lives down there, and people like you can just stay up here and watch, like gods.'

Matthew let go of her hand. He was hurt, and Gina had, in fact, meant to hurt him. She wasn't sure why.

'Like gods? That's the kind of thing that my mom would say, actually,' Matthew said after a moment, as if reasoning with himself, trying to make some sense of her rudeness. 'She would like you, you know. My mom. I think you would like her too.'

Gina smiled, her mood lightening. 'So now you want me to meet the parents?'

'As long as you introduce me to your Ma Taffy.'

Gina laughed. 'I don't think so. Ma Taffy wouldn't like you.'

'Why not?'

Gina looked Matthew up and down, thinking many thoughts but saying none of them.

'Because I'm white?' Matthew pressed.

'Something like that. It's cause you are what she calls Babylon.'

'Backside! So your aunty thinks I'm a whole Byzantine city!'

'You're part of it.'

'I'm part of Babylon?'

'You're part of the system.'

'And what does that even mean?'

'It means that people like you look down on people like Ma Taffy. Or people like me. You look down on the way we talk, the kind of clothes we wear, on everything. We too buttoo, or too cruffish, or boogooyaga, or we don't have no class. Is all a big joke. That is the system. That is Babylon.'

'I don't look down on you,' he protested, 'or the way you talk or anything.'

'Yes, but that's only cause I know how to change the way I talk when I talking to uptown people like you. If you did hear me speaking to somebody in Augustown, then I would sound different. And you would look on me different. Even though it was still me, and inside I was the same person, you would look on me different. You can't tell me that's not true.'

'It's just the way I was raised.'

'I know. It's the system. That's just how things set.'

'Well, what am I supposed to do about it, Gina? Say sorry? Find every striking person on this island that have less money than my family does and say sorry to them? *I'm so sorry that I'm white. I'm so sorry that my father makes a fuckload of money. I'm sorry that I speak good English.* Would that help?'

'Sorry wouldn't change anything. But is good to know these things.'

'Well, if it's any consolation, my mom would definitely like you, but Daddy . . . I don't think so.'

Gina laughed again. 'Because I'm black?'

Sometimes it frightened Matthew that there was such a strange and brutal and beautiful honesty between them. He had flirted with girls before, but always there was, in that flirtation, an element of flattery and deception. It was never so with Gina. And it was this honesty between them that made Matthew decide, as teenagers do, that he was more than just infatuated.

'No. Not because you're black. Because you're from down there,' and he jutted his lips out, pointing them towards Augustown.

'But that's where your mother works.'

'And they fight about it all the time. Daddy keeps on saying she could do better.'

'He's an ass.'

'But he's my dad.'

'That don't stop him being an ass.'

They went into the house after that, into Matthew's bedroom. Gina ran a finger along a shelf that boasted several water polo and swimming trophies, as if everything today wanted to remind her that she was not from this world.

They sat on the edge of his bed. Matthew offered to help her study, and there was, in fact, a bit of that. He quizzed her on the periodic table.

'H?'

'Hydrogen.'

'Au?'

'Gold.'

'T.'

'Titanium.'

She described perfectly how to perform a titration.

And then Matthew leaned in to kiss her. She kissed him back. Ma Taffy's voice came into her head suddenly. *To make a fool kiss you is one thing, but to make a kiss fool you is an even worser thing.*

'But this boy is no fool!' she said to the voice, trying to silence it. 'Sometimes he is a little naive, sure, but he is no fool.' They continued kissing for a long time.

The second time she was at his house it went further than kissing, and this thing went on for months. Sometimes when he was inside her, Gina felt again that Ma Taffy was standing right above them, her sightless eyes staring. *To make a fool fuck you is one thing, but to make a fuck fool you is an even worser thing. Don't make no man turn you into no fool.*

June came like a sadness, and Matthew was packing his bags to go off to Boston. 'Mommy and Daddy want me to go up early so I can settle in – get to know the place. It's not that I want to leave so soon.' He ran a finger from her earlobe to her chin then gently lifted her face so their eyes could meet. It was a gesture he had seen in a movie, but he did it grace-fully, as if to add a sort of pathos to his leaving.

'You don't have to explain,' Gina said, as if she too were playing a role, as if to be pragmatic and mature, although she was grateful for the explanation. In fact, for months she would replay these words in her head, this gesture. She would run her own finger along the curve of her face im-agining it was his.

Gina loved Matthew in the way that teenage girls love their first loves; which is to say, with extravagance. Whenever she saw him, she felt a beautiful hollow in her chest opening up as if it would swallow her whole being, and when she passed anyone on the street who looked anything like him she would miss a step. But she also loved him with restraint – a restraint that was not quite hers nor his, nor could it be defined exactly, though if one had to, it was perhaps the restraint of an entire island. They had met, this is true, and yet their meeting, regardless of the fact of it, was improbable. There was no context in which a girl who lived in Augustown and who went to Mona High could meet a boy who lived in Beverly Hills and who went to Campion. It required too many anomalies to coexist at once: the boy would have to have a mother who worked in Augustown, and the boy would have to be in his gap year, and it would have to start with an act of kindness, and there had to be something like a daily car ride, and there had to be something in the boy that would be attractive to the girl, and something in the girl that would be attractive to the boy, and they would each have to be curious and open, and so many other things. Gina and Matthew had met, but there was no further context in which they could continue to meet except the secret contexts they created for themselves. There was no plaza, no shop, no school barbecue, no park, no church, nothing. Love requires context, and they had none. This leaving, then, was probably for the best.

Gina thought briefly about telling him about her missed periods, but decided against it. It would transform her in his eyes. She was sure of it. She would no longer be the girl from Augustown, the bright gyal from the ghetto who defied all of his expectations. Instead she would be the girl from Augustown who confirmed them – the ghetto gyal who had tried to tie down a nice uptown boy with her belly, who had tried to rob him of his rightful future. And besides, she said to herself, she wasn't going to keep it. So what good would telling him do?

On the day before he left, Matthew held her hand. 'Gina,' he said, 'Next year you should apply. I know it might sound like an impossible thing, but you would get in. Harvard would give you a scholarship. You're bright enough.'

She said nothing. It did sound like an impossible thing. She wanted to rise out of Augustown, but she had never dreamed of rising that high. Her dreams weren't as big as uptown dreams. No. She wouldn't apply, she knew that. There would be too many details to figure out, too many hoops to jump through, too many questions to ask and not a single soul in all her world who she could ask these questions or who could point her in the right direction. And also, she thought, this was just his sweet way of saying goodbye without saying goodbye – holding out the promise that they would see each other again. It was probably his way of saying that he would miss her, when probably what she really needed was to learn how to forget him.

'So you'll apply?' he pressed. 'It doesn't even have to be Harvard. Any school in Boston, really. There's lots of them. MIT. Tufts. Boston College. You'll get in. Trust me.'

'I never even been on a plane before,' she protested.

'Not yet,' Matthew said. 'But one day. One day you're going to fly.'

24

The wind has stopped blowing. No longer can the principal or her helper hear the strains of song coming up from Augustown, the G#s and C#s carried on the end of the breeze like pollen. They have returned to sitting, and while Mrs G lowers herself onto the bench, she sighs. She has wanted so much to tell Miss G her own news: how she and Mr Garrick have decided that they will no longer be needing her services and that she, Miss G, is now to focus completely on school. What is more, Mr Garrick has agreed to fund Miss G the whole way through. His wife has strong-armed him into this position, of course. 'Think about it, Timothy,' she had said. 'Look how many companies are giving out scholarships to young people, and then when they graduate, that person is contracted to work for them. Isn't that how it works in your world? Being a good corporate citizen and all that. It's not a handout. It's an investment.'

'It's not that simple,' he had said, though it was. He just didn't like his wife meddling in his world, dictating business decisions.

'Well, I've told you, Timothy. We are going to help this girl out. We are. So either we do it using our own money, or you get your company to do it. And,' she looked at him directly, 'you owe me.'

Mr Garrick swallowed hard at these words, at the accusation. His wife hardly ever brought it up, but there it was. And this was marriage, after all; a give and take. He had made her give up teaching, the thing that had given her the greatest sense of worth, and he had done it for the sake of his own worth, his own sense of pride. Well, now she was calling in the favour. And he realised for the first time that Claudia needed this; she probably needed it more than the helper, this sense that she had helped someone to transform their life.

In the three years that Miss G had worked in their house, Mr Garrick had not grown fond of the woman. And it wasn't just her natty hair which he frankly found disgraceful and tried not to sneer at. Someone had once told him that these Rastafarian, or bobo dreads, or whatever-they-wanted-to-call-themselves, didn't even wash or shampoo, and that many of them had insects living in their great clumps of hair. It made him squeamish, and all the more incredulous that Claudia should have hired such a woman to keep their own house tidy. He would have protested, but there was no talking to Claudia in matters such as this. 'Timothy,' she would have said, had he dared, 'I have lived with all your faults, your stupid pride and even the women on the side. Don't think for a moment I have not known about them. I have lived with all of it. But I am not a snob, and I will not stand for your snobbery!' With each word, her volume would have risen, and Mr Garrick would have feared that the neighbours might overhear the altercation, which in turn would hurt his pride even more deeply. So he had left it alone. But it was also the damned haughtiness of this helper, a quality he couldn't quite put his finger on. It was the way she walked this high-assed walk, but with a kind of prudishness, as if no man was supposed to try and check her out; and it was the way she had taken down every blasted book off his shelves, his books – books he hadn't read himself and probably never would read, and had read them from cover to cover, when she should have waited her turn; and it was the way he observed her observing things, this damn woman who couldn't afford one thing in their house, not one thing, and yet she looked at the rugs, the paintings, the walls, everything, as if she was assessing it, and sometimes didn't quite approve. Oh, how it rankled with him! The fact that she was doing so well under Claudia's tutelage only confirmed what he disliked about her. He would never say such a thing out loud, not to anyone, yet it seemed to him that here was a young woman who did not know her place. But what to do? They had gone so far down this road, and he could see no way to get himself out of it now.

'All right, I will talk to the fellows at the office, see if we can do something,' he had said to his wife. And to give Timothy Garrick his due, he did say something to his finance director the next morning, though he also tried to sabotage the plans by being absolutely honest about the whole thing. 'This is just the helper, Jimmy. Claudia has a thing for her and is trying to help her out. You see what I mean? Don't get me wrong. She's quite bright, this girl, but at the end of the day she's just the helper, goddammit. Anyway, I thought I'd put it out there because, well, I promised Claudia I'd see what I could do. But I told her these things are difficult at the best of times. So don't put yourself under any pressure.'

211

But the finance director had not properly understood Mr Garrick. He dutifully said something to the HR manager, and impressed upon her that this request was coming from the big boss himself; the HR manager in turn said something to the PR manager. The PR manager was a woman whose enthusiasm for just about everything grated on Mr Garrick, but who was so good at her job that he was forced to tolerate her. She came back to Mr Garrick beaming. 'What a story, Mr Garrick!' she enthused. 'What an incredible story! It's gold! Absolute gold! We are going to get so much mileage out of this, I promise you.'

Mr Garrick felt his heart go flat.

'Can you imagine?' The PR manager continued, and spread her arms as if to present the future in headlines. 'Front page material: "Helper From Augustown Aces A Levels". Oh, that's good! And with help from your wife, no less, is that what they're telling me, that your wife was the one who taught her? That's really good. "Helper Gets Into UWI"! And then, "Helper From Augustown First Recipient Of Garrick Foundation Scholarship"! That's what we should call it. What you think, Mr Garrick? It has a ring to it, no?'

Mr Garrick frowned. 'The company is Garrick Enterprises,' he said grumpily. 'We don't have a foundation.'

'Minor matters, sir! Minor! We can even start a foundation now. Easy-peasy. But "Garrick Enterprises Scholarship"? Mm-mm. No – that's not warm enough for what we want. You see what I mean?'

He tried another tactic. 'Yes, but if we give this too much press, aren't you worried people will find the whole thing, well, a bit nepotistic?'

'Oh no, sir! Not in a bad way. I mean, this young woman

212

isn't family to you. You have no connection to her. She's just the helper. A diamond in the rough that you managed to find. And besides, she will just be the first. This is a real opportunity for us, Mr Garrick. We should give a scholarship every year, or every two years, to some other disadvantaged youth or other. You see what I mean?'

'I see.'

'Oh, Mr Garrick . . . it will be the story of the year for us. Amazing!'

So this is the news that Mrs G wants to share with Miss G. If this university letter confirms what they both know it will confirm, then things are about to change for the helper. The PR manager has been working overtime, and already the *Gleaner* wants an interview. But that news will have to wait. Miss G is determined to open the letter not in Beverly Hills but in Augustown, in the presence of Ma Taffy and Kaia. Though disappointed, Mrs G understands this reasoning.

'All right, Miss G,' she says finally, standing up and patting her pockets to feel for her car keys. 'Let me at least give you a ride down the hill so you can get home a little quicker.'

'Thank you, Mrs G. I would appreciate that.'

213

25

Come. Let us observe it now, the autoclaps. Begin in Beverly Hills. See how the blue Honda makes its way down the bumpy hill. And was anything ever more innocent than this, a simple car driving on a simple road? At the bottom of the hill it takes a right onto Monroe Road, Monroe Road that soon becomes the long curve of Wellington Drive, the road like a closed parabola. At the end of Wellington Drive, the car takes a right onto Mona Road and drives its full length, past the once tidy Mona suburbs on the left, Mona High School and the hockey field on the right, and then under the old cut-stone plantation aqueduct, and then past the old plantation itself, which is, of course, no longer a plantation but the University of the West Indies. But now, as we approach Augustown, we lose the car under a copse of trees and yellow flowers.

Zoom in, then.

'Right here is fine,' says Miss G.

So Mrs G pulls the car up beside the kerb. 'I love this time of year,' she says, dipping her head to look out of the car and up to the trees that grow along the pavement. 'The exam trees are flowering.' By this, she means the poui trees. There is a saying on the university campus, *When the pouis appear, exams are near*, and indeed the trees are beginning to throw their batches of yellow flowers all over the road. It really is quite a beautiful harbinger.

Miss G opens the car door to let herself out, but Mrs G reaches over to hold her arm for a moment. 'Miss G, I just need to say what a pleasure it has been teaching you . . . well,' she laughs a little, 'in the end, I haven't taught you so much at all. I've just facilitated what your mind can do. But that has been a pleasure as well, just watching you accomplish things so easily.'

Miss G reaches around with her free hand and clasps Mrs G's hand. She nods and then says suddenly, 'My boy-child, Kaia. I will bring him up to the house tomorrow. You should meet him.'

Mrs G smiles. 'Yes, I would like that.' And with this they part. Mrs G turns the car around, and Miss G watches as the blue car becomes smaller and smaller until there is no car at all, just the road and the yellow flowers. Alone now under the poui tree, the helper feels herself transforming from the person of Miss G back into the person of Gina. It is only now that her heart starts to race. As Miss G, she does not feel very much. Miss G is a woman who keeps so much inside her. Miss G is a woman with secrets. But as Gina she allows herself to feel buoyant. She feels the exciting future not somewhere out there, but inside her own body, a certain lightness of being that could even allow her to float. It is beginning to spread inside her veins, this floating feeling, as if she could close her eyes right now and begin to rise, up, up, up into the air.

She thinks about the letter from the university, the university that she can turn to look on right now. She almost squeals. It is one of those moments you feel the need to pause, to touch the ground, to breathe in deeply, to take it all in, to make a memory or even a monument – this pivotal moment when you feel your whole world turning.

But the world has turned for her before, at this very spot, under one of these very trees. She did not know it at the time. It was that morning when Matthew stopped behind her and she had cursed him before she saw him, and then felt embarrassed, and then he had given her a ride to school. She did not know then that tiny moments change wide futures, that small axes fell big trees, that some days have more roads than others and some roads more distance. How appropriate, she thinks suddenly. How strikingly appropriate! It was Mrs G's blue Honda that had picked her up six years ago and carried her away from the future she had imagined for herself, and it is that same blue Honda that has just now returned her to it.

She does not regret her life. No. Let us be more specific; she does not regret Kaia. So many early mornings since his birth she has woken up in the dark in a cold sweat. She wakes up thinking of that other morning, the morning when he was born, and how she had held him over the toilet bowl, how she had almost stopped his life before it had really begun. It shames her, this memory. And it always comes back to her at the exact hour, pulling her from sleep. Is this what they call a blood memory? As if, at 2.35 each morning, a murderous intent still pulses through her heart, or an echo of something she never actually did.

When this memory comes back to her she lifts herself out of her bed and walks over to sit on the edge of Kaia's small cot. She strokes his hair and wonders if there is some part of his unconscious being that knows this evil thing that his mother almost did to him. It is possible. She has read before about the vast chambers of the mind – how sometimes it remembers things it has no business remembering. But she thinks if there really is a part of his unconscious that knows the evil that faced him at his birth, maybe there is also a part of his unconscious that has forgiven her.

Gina tries to be a good mother. She has vowed to protect him. She believes she owes him this. Ma Taffy does not always approve. She says, 'Give the boy some space, Gina. Give him room to grow his own backbone.' But how heavy is the weight of love, and how much heavier when it springs from a place of guilt.

On those dark mornings when Gina wakes up, she eventually goes down on her knees, the way women for years have gone down on their knees, and she whispers into Kaia's ears, 'You are worth it.' It sounds like a prayer, or a chant over his life.

And she really does believe this. She believes everything has been worth it. Meeting Matthew was worth it. And losing him; and dropping out of high school without a single subject; and being a simple domestic helper these last three years. It has been hard, of course. In the days following Kaia's birth she would walk through Augustown with her head down, and the boys would sit there on the fence like high court judges and look on her, coy smiles on their lips, and she would suffer the weight of their contempt. *See it there!* She knew that was what they were thinking. *See it there! You did gwaan like you was better than we. You say it right to we face that you was better than we. But look at you now. The higher monkey climb the more him batty expose. Ma Taffy never teach you that lesson? Eh? Well,*

217

see it there now! You learn it. And you couldn't learn that from no goddamn book. You always act like your shit could make patty, like you did make to eat from high table but now you eating so-so scraps like the rest of we. But the days turned into weeks and into months and into years, and she has learnt how to lift her head up and how to meet the gaze of these boys with a look that says simply, Yes. I have learnt my lessons. And then a look that says something even larger and warmer and without judgement; a look that makes the boys ashamed and causes them to look away from her. So Gina believes it has been worth it, because Kaia is worth it. Because she has learnt things these six years, it is true, that she could not have learnt from books or with her brain. She has learnt heart lessons. Love lessons. She has grown up. She is only twenty-one but already she feels like a big, big woman.

Standing now under the poui tree, Gina closes her eyes and takes a breath in order to make a memory of this moment. She can smell what Ma Taffy had smelt hours ago – the mangoes and the cherries and the otaheite apples ripening together, and then all the vague but distinct everyday smells of Augustown: coal fires burning, turn cornmeal turning, crack rice boiling, the sweat of blackwomen standing over pots, the sweat of blackmen standing in the streets. But does she smell the sweet, choking smell behind it all? Does she smell what is coming?

No. She does not. She can hear it, though – the singing and chanting that seems to come from the primary school – yet she does not pay it much attention. Her fingers curl around the fat envelope. It is time, she thinks. So she walks now towards the house. And was anything ever more innocent than this – a simple woman walking on a simple lane?

The lane does not feel emptier than usual, and Gina does not notice the few passers-by who look at her with a sense of expectation. She comes at last to the house, and up there on the verandah she sees Ma Taffy and beside the old woman, a boy. For half a second she does not recognise the boy – or she recognises him the way we recognise people in dreams who sometimes wear different faces. She closes her eyes. She opens them again. Instead of a floating feeling, she feels a sudden flatness in her being. Just so. How a day can change just so. Her fingers are curling around the envelope in her hand. And then a shivering comes. A shivering rage. She remembers herself as a three-year-old girl, and the body of Clarky hanging under the mango tree. Did the breeze make the body swing like a pendulum, or did it remain perfectly still? She cannot quite remember. But she thinks of Kaia's body, hanged. Who would want to hang her boy?

Ma Taffy is standing up. 'Gina,' she says. 'Gina, come here and let we talk this thing through.'

But Gina does not move from the spot where she is standing, and Kaia is running to her, his arms open. He is crying again. No. Not just crying. He is bawling, as if he has been saving it up all this time. It is a loud wailing sound – a cry that is not weak at all, but has backbone. And this time Gina does not tell him to stop as she usually does, but lifts him up into her arms and holds him close.

'I . . . never do nothing . . . Mommy! I wasn't . . . rude . . . or nothing!' He explains himself through snot and tears and hiccups. 'Is Mr . . . Saint-Josephs . . . cut . . . off my hair. And I . . . wasn't even rude or nothing . . . Mommy!'

She kisses his cheek. It tastes of salt.

'Gina?' Ma Taffy says. 'Gina.'

Still Gina does not respond. She lifts Kaia away from her and puts him back on the ground.

'I soon come back,' she says.

'Gina?' Ma Taffy calls to her, but Gina is already walking away, back through the lane, through the streets that are named as if marking a calendar – August Road, July Street, June Boulevard. She walks towards the school.

The crowd by the school gate is not as big now as it was an hour ago. One by one people have left; they have other things to do, other people to meet, goods to sell before the day is fully done, pots left on fires that need tending. They have also been told that old Sister Gilzene has died, so there is the funeral home to call, the body to move, the mattress to turn over and the furniture to rearrange so that the duppy won't come back and haunt them. Also, Ma Taffy hasn't come to join them with the boy. They had hoped she would. It would have given them more purpose – they could have held the boy and hugged him and wept over him and felt a greater sense of anger on his behalf. The teacher is also nowhere to be seen. They imagine he is cowering in some corner of the schoolyard. But without the teacher, and without the boy, there is nothing for them to group up against or group up in support of. After a while, the big feeling that set them marching and chanting at the gate feels a little foolish, the whole thing about the boy and his hair being cut just another unfortunate incident – spilt milk, really; nothing that affects the price of bread – so one by one they return to their lives.

As Gina walks the last stretch towards the school she does

not pay attention to the people walking past her. But they notice her. They notice how she holds herself tight but her whole body is shivering. They notice how each of her steps presses an incredible anger into the ground, and how the white dust from the marl road rises up in little bursts and sprinkles on her feet. They run back towards the school. 'Mama coming!' one of them shouts, and something is re-ignited, an energy that had dissipated; the focus they needed has finally arrived. Before, they were a hurricane without a centre. Now they can be pelting rain and gale force wind and red skies. They can be destruction and calamity and the bruggalungdung. They begin bellowing for the teacher again. 'Send him out! Send him out! Make him answer to Mama!' They hold on to the gate and on to the fence and shake them.

The woman whose job it is each evening to sweep and mop the classrooms of Augustown Primary, and who is still lingering outside classroom 2B, hears the rattling of the gate and the fence. She hears the loud bang as they are torn down. She hisses to her dog, 'Jeeezas Chrise, Jack Sprat! That sound like autoclaps!'

26

Consider the crowd – the phenomenon of the 'twelfth man' in English football – the way a crowd can bring out the best in a single player, how they can whoop and cheer their teams on to victory, but how they can also infect a single person with false feelings: anonymity; invulnerability; inherent morality; a reduced sense of responsibility. It is also the crowd that riots, that loots, that lynches – it is the crowd that bays for blood.

So although Gina is so much inside her own self, inside her own anger, that she does not acknowledge the crowd, she is still a part of it – she is its epicentre. She feeds on its energy, and the crowd feeds on hers. No one here is an individual. Every man and woman is an extension of Gina. Even Bongo Moody, in this moment, is not quite himself, but an angry mother.

In the almost twenty years since that evening when Clarky was found under the tree, Gina has not talked to Bongo Moody or met his eyes when they have passed each other in the road. To meet those eyes would be to face something neither of them wants to face, or something they do not even know how to face – the guilt of being small in this world and unable to stop terrible things from happening.

But in this moment Gina meets Bongo Moody's eyes, and his anger is a mirror of her own. *It come back to this,* she says to him with her eyes, and he agrees, *Yes, it has come back to this.*

And then something passes between them. She does not say out loud, 'Tear down the fence! Open the bloodclawt gate!' but he says it for her. 'Tear down the fence!' and so the crowd that is an extension of Gina pulls and pushes and tears down the barrier because this is what she wants. The gate crashes to the ground.

Gina walks into the school. The crowd follows behind her. Now they are patting her back, literally pushing her forward, egging her on with, 'Wicked thing de teacherman do to your boy, Mama! Wicked thing!'

'Yes! Go deal with him case now. The wicked brute!'

'Dem fi lef people pickney alone! After a nuh dem birth nuhbady. Dem too evilous and carry-down!'

She goes to the staff room. It is empty.

She walks around the compound to the building with the classrooms.

Classroom 1A . . . Empty.

1B . . . Empty.

1C . . . Empty.

2A . . . Empty.

Classroom 2B.

Mr Saint-Josephs is standing there. His trousers, a size too small, squeeze his large thighs and his stomach strains at the white shirt which he has tucked deeply into the trousers. His afro is untidy and his round face is wet with sweat, but his expression is completely blank.

'Ma'am, what can I do for you?' he asks, a strange stoicism in his voice.

223

The crowd is gathered behind Gina but they are quiet now.

Gina does not need to ask if this is the teacher she is looking for, because on the floor there is still the evidence of his crime – her son's dreadlocks, lifeless. On the edge of the teacher's table, the rusty scissors he used to cut the locks. She bends down and gathers the hair into the cup of her hands and now she is also crying.

'Is you name Mr Saint-Josephs?'

'Ma'am, what can I do for you?' Mr Saint-Josephs asks again, but now he has turned his face to look above the heads of the crowd out into the schoolyard.

'Sir, I want to know why you do this thing to mi son? What him do to you?'

'That little hooligan,' Mr Saint-Josephs whispers, but still his eyes are not on her and his voice is hollow and far away.

The seeming indifference hurts Gina. She begins to tremble even more. Her eyes are red. Her mouth tastes of salt. She raises her voice. 'Mr Saint-Josephs, sir. I asking you a simple question, please. Why you do this to my boy? What him do to you? You understand nothing bout the Nazirite vows? You know nothing bout Rasta?'

'Ungroomed little hooligan,' Mr Saint-Josephs says. It is a version of the speech he has practised for the principal. 'But is not even their fault you know, ma'am. The parents are to blame. Sending them to school so unkempt and nasty with that picky-picky hairstyle. If you ask me, I did the boy a favour. For look at his skin. Look at his high colour. He could be a big somebody in this country, but he making out like him is a little bush African.'

Mr Saint-Josephs is a big man, tall and wide, but Gina

224

doesn't seem to notice this. She lifts her hands to grab him by his shirt collar, and the crowd is now excited. 'Lick him, Mama! Lick de brute! Him out-a-order though!'

The woman whose job it is each evening to mop out the classrooms, who stands aside from the crowd, unobserved, holds the imaginary dog, Jack Sprat, closer to her chest.

'Slut!' Mr Saint-Josephs says, still not looking at Gina despite her small hands clutching his shirt collar. 'Raasclawt slut!' and now he too is crying. 'You raasclawt whore. How you could do this to me?!'

And Gina is remembering Ma Taffy's words from an early morning so many years ago. *Wicked bloodclawt whore of Babylon! Dutty Jezebel gyal! What could really make you think of doing such a thing? Eeeh? To kill off yu own little baby? That is murder! That is wickedness.*

Gina and Mr Saint-Josephs, lost for a moment in their own histories. The past, when it takes hold of us, does not let go easily. But Gina hears when Mr Saint-Josephs grunts, and she lets go of him, moving her face just before his fist slams into it. The crowd moves in. Gina thinks again of Ma Taffy's words. *Learn how to use the tools of Babylon against Babylon*, and now she notices the rusty scissors on the edge of the desk. Was there ever more a tool of Babylon than this? She reaches for the scissors. The crowd draws its breath. Gina pulls her hand back and then throws it forward. She sinks the pair of scissors into Mr Saint-Josephs' left eye. It pops. Blood shoots out from the eye socket and splashes the crowd. Everyone is shielding their eyes and screaming. The cleaning woman is running away, holding her imaginary dog and screaming. Emanuel Saint-Josephs is screaming the loudest even as Gina pulls the scissors from his eye and it makes a sloppy wet

225

sound. He bends over, holding the place where his eye once was, trying to stop the bleeding.

At last the crowd dissolves into separate people, no longer an extension of Gina. The deed done, they want no part of it, and now there is a muttering. 'Jeezas Chrise, she shouldna did do it! I don't know is what fly up into her head, suh!'

But Gina hears none of this. She turns around and the shocked group of witnesses parts. She walks between them. She wants to get back home. In one hand she holds the pair of scissors, in the other, the dreadlocks she has gathered from the floor.

The cleaning woman, who has now taken shelter in the staff room, is on the phone with Mrs G. She has been given instructions to call the principal in case of any emergency, but she has done this once too often for the principal's liking. Once it was because CIA agents had surrounded the school; another time because Patti LaBelle was giving a concert and acting rude. Mrs G is therefore sceptical at first, but she also remembers that when the cleaning lady called about the CIA agents and about Patti LaBelle, she did not sound overly anxious − not the way she sounds now.

'It awful here, Mrs G! It awful. Blood everywhere!'

'What is awful? What's happening?'

'Lawd dem do the teacherman bad, ma'am. Stab him up! Oh God.'

'Who has stabbed who? The CIA?'

'What kinda CIA you talking bout ma'am?! No! The people dem from Augustown. Them tear the gate down and come in and stab up the teacherman.'

'Which teacherman?'

'The big, swarthy fool-fool one in 2B, ma'am.'

And now Mrs G knows the cleaning lady is telling the truth.

'Yes, ma'am. One lady just take up something and stab him. Blood everywhere! Mi not touching it, ma'am. No. Mi not cleaning that up.'

'Look. I want you to stay right there. I'm calling the police and I'll come down immediately.'

'Yes, ma'am. Cause it awful down here now. Awful.'

Gina is taking step by slow step – around the school compound, over the fallen gate and now through the streets that are like markings on a calendar. The sun is lowering itself, and Augustown is bathed in the red light of evening. While it is roosters that announce the morning, it is the parakeets that announce the evening. They fill the Augustown sky, flying from mango tree to mango tree and dropping their green feathers on the ground. They screech what sounds almost like a song:

Evening time, work is over now is evening time!

The rhythm of the whole place changes. Women sit outside on concrete blocks with clips and baubles between their teeth as they comb the hair of little girls, who wince and will have to wear stocking caps to bed so that the hair is in place come morning. The little boys are freer – they play in the road in only their underwear and thin vests, running hose-wheels with stretched-out clothes hangers or bouncing a football between them.

Everyone stops to stare at Gina, though she isn't sure what they are looking at. She doesn't feel odd with the dreadlocks held like a bouquet in one hand or the bloody scissors still in the other. What she feels is nothing, but a kind of

227

nothing that is full of everything, the way the colour black is full of every colour, which is to say that she suddenly feels herself as cavernous as a place in which things can find an echo and a resonance, so the nothingness that she feels is loud and full. What she feels, if she could name it, is that same floating feeling coursing through her veins. What she feels is the colour red of evening. What she feels is the parakeets and their feathers. What she feels is the cracked road, and the zinc fences still graffitied with 'JLP' and 'NO TO COMMUNISSM'.

She is almost back at Ma Taffy's house. She does not hear the police jeep behind her, how its wheels crush the gravel. She does not hear the policeman with his bullhorn telling her to *stop, stop now ma'am and put your hands in the air!* She does not see how the boys in just their underwear and vests are running inside, following the women from the concrete blocks who have grabbed their daughters to drag them in as well. She does not hear the policeman on his bullhorn again saying, *Drop the weapon, lady. You must listen when police talk to you! You fi bloodclawt drop the weapon and put yu hands in the air!*

No. She does not hear any of it. She only sees Ma Taffy running off the verandah towards her. And she wonders why. Why should Ma Taffy run like that? And she can't even see! Suppose she should stumble? She feels like laughing. She wants to say, Ma Taffy! Have you forgotten your age papers? And Kaia is running towards her as well.

She does not hear the first gunshot, fired as a warning, and she does not feel the second, fired by another policeman who thinks the first shot means it is open season. Neither does she feel the third. But how could the day smell so much of jackfruit just so, she wonders. The stinking, clawing

228

stench of an overripe jackfruit that has fallen to the floor and burst open. And why is Ma Taffy now falling to her knees – falling the way so many mothers have fallen to their knees for years? And why is her face twisted in such pain? *What is wrong, Ma Taffy?* She wants to ask. *Why so downcast, oh my soul?*

And Kaia is in front of her. She wants to reach out and pick him up. But now she feels herself falling. She feels herself draining from herself. She thinks, I have been poured out like water. Kaia seems to be shouting, 'Mommy! Mommy!' but though she sees his lips move, she does not hear him. She thinks, *Yes. I am Mommy. Your own mommy who will never let nobody trouble you. My name is Gina Elizabeth McDonald. Miss G to others. I am the bright gyal from the ghetto who going to rise out of this shit hole. Yes, Kaia. We going to rise out of here.* She thinks, *I am the Dispenser and the Watchman; I am the Shepherd and the Trumpeter. I am the flying woman.*

And she thinks . . . and she thinks . . . and every thought is like an echo of something else, of a terrible history. Her mind is the red evening sky, a vast chamber full of green birds and wings. And she thinks, and she floats.

And she falls.

27

You will not find the body, which you may find incredible, or incredulous, but perhaps it is time at last to make space in yourself to believe such stories, and to believe the people who tell them. Go now then, back down to earth and then to Augustown; sit on a verandah and just be still. Just listen. It would be best, perhaps, if you go to the house that once belonged to Ma Taffy and where she once lived with Gina and Kaia. Ma Taffy is dead now, of course, of natural causes. But at that house they will remember her.

Now let the night settle into all the corners of that dismal little valley. Let the mongrel dogs settle into the potholes where they sleep. Let the music of speaker boxes play some sweet reggae music and let the guns bark. Let the men seated around the corner shop slap their dominoes on the table. Let everything find its rhythm, and then wait for someone – another old woman, perhaps – to turn her face towards the hillside that still wears its scar. Wait for a kind of remembrance to begin:

You remember Soft-Paw? Him was the first real badman from Augustown. Marlon was him rightful name. And him had a talent to just creep up on you and you don't hear a thing. We all did think that it was Babylon that would kill him one day, but it wasn't. It was him own people that do him in, throw the body over there in Mona Dam with concrete block chain up round him.

And remember Sister Gilzene — the one who did sing so beautiful? She dead on the same day when all that autoclaps did come to Augustown.

Lawd have mercy, yes! You remember that autoclaps?

The police left quickly that evening. After Gina fell, there was a sudden quiet that was not a peaceful kind of quiet. No. This was the quiet of old and hungry tigers that knew they still had within themselves the strength to pounce. Doors started to open and people walked into the streets, their backs upright, their shoulders squared, looking straight at the police — the police who knew this time to feel a little afraid because they did not have muscle enough to fight this.

After the police left, the schoolboys of Augustown tied together the laces of their old sneakers and threw them up high into the air until they caught over the electric wires — the wires that run from post to post, like Calvary repeating itself on every street. And why do they do this strange ritual, this throwing of the shoes whenever someone has been shot down? No one can tell you exactly. Maybe it is to create a path in the air, a suggestion to the dead that up there is where they should be walking.

The police left the body in the street. Ma Taffy went inside and came back out with white sheets. She wrapped Gina's body with them and then neighbours helped her to lift the body out of the road and lay it down again in her front yard.

They blocked the roads that night. They dragged old fridges and stoves and tyres and sheets of zinc into the streets. They poured kerosene oil and set fire to it all. Black smoke rose into the sky and Augustown was hedged in by this burning. JBC-TV news and RJR radio reported that there was great unrest in the troubled community – that residents of Mona and Hope Pastures and Beverly Hills should exercise caution.

Still, at least one woman who lived up there in Beverly Hills was trapped in Augustown that night.

Remember her? Mrs G. The principal lady. I believe the G did stand for Garrick. Good woman, that. I still see her now and then. Age catch up with her a little bit, though.

Mrs G had gone back to the school. She had waited for an ambulance to come and take Mr Saint-Josephs off to the hospital.

The teacher? Is him they call Oney now?

Yes – him same one.

The one-eyed madman is one of Papine's regulars – a filthy, barefoot beggar whose hair has clumped into three magnificent locks. He wears a dirty patch over his left eye, but hardly anything else, so his long, crusted penis is often seen dangling by his knees while he walks about. The one-eyed madman sleeps on a bench in the middle of Papine Square. He does not sleep on a sheet of old newspapers, or on a pillow of cardboard boxes – just himself on the bare bench with the warm Jamaican night wrapped around him. If the square is his bedroom, then the street is his toilet. If you are in Papine early one morning, you might be so unlucky as to see the one-eyed madman squatting by the traffic lights, positioning himself over an open drain, a thick braid of shit pushing its way out of his body. For this, the one-eyed madman has had the foulest words and the largest stones thrown at him; he has been chased away, even by cars. Sometimes he runs towards Gordon Town and further up to the Blue Mountains, but always by nightfall Oney returns to bed down on his bench. By nightfall people will have forgotten the nauseating sight of his excrement, or they will have forgiven him. He is just another madman, after all. But because he is a madman, no one knows how to acknowledge the fact that they need him — that his presence gives an order and a sense and a balance to their days. It is almost certain that in the year that Oney dies, the people of Papine will walk around for months nursing an emptiness that they will not be able to explain. They will not care to know that the one-eyed madman's leaving has upset their equilibrium so greatly.

On the evening when this man stopped being Mr Saint-Josephs and became instead the one-eyed madman, Mrs G stayed back after seeing him off in the ambulance. It was she who mopped out the classroom, then rearranged the desks in a neat and tidy order. By now the sun was down, and the crickets were chirping innocently, and she sat at one of the desks and cried. In the classroom she blamed herself, for on his very first day of teaching Mr Saint-Josephs had stormed into her office. Should this have been a sign to her? And after he had left, Mrs G had stared at the door and thought to herself, 'This is not a man to be teaching young children.' Yes, she had actually had that precise thought, and so it was this that came back to accuse her. She wept.

The minute hand on her watch had spun around the dial twice before she decided it was finally time for her to go — that Mr Garrick would be at home, worried. She drove out of the school, but soon found that every road in Augustown was blocked, hedged in by fire. She made no fuss about this. She parked the car, stepped out of it and into the warm night of Augustown. It wrapped itself around her in a welcoming

233

way. The night seemed to tell her that she was a part of this.

Mrs G walked, and she walked until she found the lane where candles had been lit all the way down and shoes had been thrown over the overhead wires. She walked up to Ma Taffy's verandah, where the old woman was sitting in absolute silence, the boy Kaia weeping into her lap.

'Welcome,' Ma Taffy said. Mrs G nodded and took a seat herself. There would be a time for these two women to talk, but that time was not now.

In the streets they had set up some big speaker boxes and they played sweet music throughout the night. The Tamlins singing 'Baltimore', and Bunny Wailer making them Rock and Groove, and J. C. Lodge reminding them that somebody loved them.

Oh Lord, you remember those tunes? Now them was singers!

There wasn't any great outpouring of sadness. Nobody read a Bible verse. Nobody offered any remembrance or any impromptu eulogy. No one went up to Ma Taffy and Kaia or Mrs G to tell them how sorry they were, and how everything was going to be OK. No. It wasn't going to be OK, and it wasn't that sort of night. They were just easy together. Sitting out in the streets and drinking rum and Red Stripe beer, and all the time the body was just lying there in the yard, wrapped up in the white sheets.

It was getting close to midnight. Then Ma Taffy got up, just like that, and said, 'Turn it off. Turn off the music.' There was a great shuffle to do this. The lane slipped into a sudden silence. Ma Taffy descended the stairs and went into the yard. She drew Kaia along with her. They stood over the body. Ma Taffy began to sing.

Hers was not the best singing voice. It was old and crackly

and could not stay on any one note. It didn't matter. She sang. Mrs G went over to join them, as if she were family, and she put one hand around Kaia and the other hand she stretched out. That's when the body began to move.

No one gasped. No one fainted. It was that sort of night. It was a night when such things seemed like the most normal thing in the world. More people were now joining in on the song. Who could offer a descant offered her descant, and who could offer a bass offered his bass, and who could offer a tenor offered his tenor, and so on.

Just like that, a thing will rise up into the air. And so they sang. The body rose off of the ground. They sang some more. They sang until the body was floating above them, wrapped in its white sheets. Now everyone was lifting their hands up to the heavens. The body just kept rising and rising as if it wanted to join the crowded sky.

On the night of the autoclaps, the sky was velvet blue. A sliver of moon was shining.

The body rose, the sheets billowing about it. It grew smaller with distance. It soon looked like a white bird up there, flapping its wings. The bird oared the night air. It circled around Augustown. It squawked.

Then the bird began to beat its wings harder. It rose even further up into the sky. It rose so high that it soon became just a dot of white light.

And they will tell you that this is where she is right now, risen up there in the heavens, in a section of the night sky that overlooks the vast sands of the dry river and the poui trees and the zinc fences and the lanes than run in untidy directions; that overlooks Kintyre and 'Gola and Dread Heights and Armagiddeon Yard. Up there is sky and emptiness, though such emptiness depends on human presumption, a terrestrial idea of scale and distance. In fact, there are many things up there, many kinds of stars: pulsars, quasars, white dwarfs and red giants. There are asteroids and meteoroids and comets and dust. Up there, there is water – endless lakes of it – enough to drown the earth a million times over. And there are clouds that taste of raspberries and that smell of rum; and planets of ice and planets of diamond; and at least a dozen dogs and chimpanzees – the remains of failed space missions, their carcasses forever floating about in space. Up there is the Lion of Judah, the black god, Marcus Garvey, Bedward, Emmanuel-I, Selassie-I, Jah Rastafari. And these are just the things we have names for.

Gina? That person that once was me. I am none of these things – not asteroid, not star, not angel. I have become something else. I am just another 'Once Upon A Time', another 'Crick Crack', another 'Quiet as it's kept', another Invisible Man, or perhaps Woman; just another voice without a mouth; another consciousness without a human body; another story pulsing its intermittent light among the galaxies. I am floating.

But wouldn't you like to be me? For what is more human than this, the desire to escape the troubled earth and its depressing gravity? What is more human than the desire to rise above it all, to fly?

Down there is Augustown. 17° 59' 0" North, 76° 44' 0" West. It sits between two hillsides, and one of these carries on its face a scar – a scar that feels to many as if they wear it on their own skin. Down there they look up each night to see me and imagine that one day I will return, more dreadful than ever, with lightning in my hands and with judgement

236

to mete out on Babylon. If only it were so! But it is not. It is not so. I am simply here, up here, another nameless thing in the sky.

Thanks

The words of poets are powerful, even when they don't intend them to be, and this novel has been powered by the words of two poets who deserve special thanks: Ishion Hutchinson, who once told me the story of the teacher who cut off his dreadlocks when he was just a small boy in Jamaica; and the venerable poet/historian Professor Kamau Brathwaite, who once, breaking from the script of a distinguished lecture he had been giving, looked into the audience and issued this instruction: 'It is time to write about Bedward.'

Thanks also go out to the Jamaica Rhodes Trust and the Rex Nettleford Fellowship in Cultural Studies, which gave me space and funds to write this book; to Shaun Champion and Katie McIntosh, who read early drafts of this manuscript; to my friends Scarlett Beharie and Kaschief Johnson, who believed in this book even when most of it was still only in my head; to my agents Alice and Alice, who share not only a name but also a propensity for magic; to my ever-faithful editor, Kirsty, and my old family at Weidenfeld & Nicolson; and to my new family at Knopf/Random House.

blog and newsletter

For literary discussion, author insight,
book news, exclusive content,
recipes and giveaways, visit the
Weidenfeld & Nicolson blog and
sign up for the newsletter at:

www.wnblog.co.uk

For breaking news, reviews and exclusive competitions
Follow us 🐦 @wnbooks
Find us 📘 facebook.com/WNfiction